To: The Minister of the Interior

From: ~~Paul Windham~~ *Stassney Murdock*

RE: New Species Discovered:
        Homo Agronomistus Arrogantus

Habitat: Islands, jungles, beaches, lagoons, other exotic locales attractive to serious agronomists

Markings: Eyes bluer than a summer sky, dark hair, a wicked grin, handsome as sin

Noted Characteristics: An unfailing honesty, an abiding sense of honor, a deep-rooted devotion to duty, also stubborn, mulish and pigheaded

Recommendation: Observe daily for foreseeable future

MEN at WORK

—MILLIONAIRE'S CLUB   —BOARDROOM BOYS   —MAGNIFICENT MEN
—TALL, DARK & SMART   —DOCTOR, DOCTOR   —MEN OF THE WEST
—MEN OF STEEL   —MEN IN UNIFORM

MEN at WORK
LAURIE PAIGE
A SEASON FOR BUTTERFLIES

TALL, DARK
AND SMART
E=MC

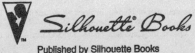

Silhouette Books

Published by Silhouette Books
America's Publisher of Contemporary Romance

SILHOUETTE BOOKS
300 East 42nd St.,
New York, N. Y. 10017

ISBN 0-373-81035-0

A SEASON FOR BUTTERFLIES

Printed in U.S.A.

Dear Reader,

For me, stories usually come about as the result of a clash between two opposing issues. In the case of Paul and Stassney, it was his concept of her easy life against the actuality of his circumstances. His former fiancée hadn't been able to tolerate his career of helping people make a living from their land. How can he expect Stassney, who comes from a private girls' school background, to adjust to sometimes living in a hut or even a tent? He can't. The problem is making her face the truth about that. Heck, any man picked at random on the street can tell you how stubborn females are.

What Paul, smart as he is, doesn't realize is that most women are a lot more adaptable than his ex-fiancée had been. After all, women were the first gatherers, then sowers and harvesters. Any woman of sense could have told him that. Besides, we've been packing up the kids and traveling with our men to the ends of the earth for centuries. Living in a hut is hard? So what else is new?

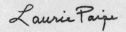

Please address questions and book requests to:
Silhouette Reader Service
U.S.: 3010 Walden Ave., P.O. Box 1325, Buffalo, NY 14269
Canadian: P.O. Box 609, Fort Erie, Ont. L2A 5X3

Chapter One

Stassney Murdock was normally good-natured. She had come into the world as a good-natured baby, rarely given to tantrums, and when she did explode, it was only under duress. As a child, her lively curiosity had been the culprit most responsible for getting her into trouble. At the present moment, she was somewhat worried. And more than a little tired.

Lifting a hand to brush the reddish-brown feathery bangs off her perspiring forehead, she noticed the tremor in her fingers that indicated her unusually long day, the fourth in a series of long days.

Four days ago, she had left her home in Connecticut and had flown to Australia, then to Port Moresby, the capital city of Papua New Guinea. From there, she had caught an island shuttle flight to Boang Island of the Tanga Island group where she had waited overnight for the cargo-passenger ship that had finally deposited her at the island of Lyra after a slow ten-hour voyage.

Dusk was fast approaching and no one had come for her. Where was the plantation manager that Leah had promised would be on hand to take her to the house?

Stassney brought her shaky hand to lips that echoed the tremble of weariness. The ship blew several short blasts from its steam whistle as it moved away from the wharf. Stassney's stomach, still queasy from seasickness, heaved itself into a knot of fear. She tried to relax. Someone will come, she assured her flagging spirits.

"About time," she muttered as she spied a four-wheel drive vehicle coming down the dirt track that served as the main road—the only road as far as she could see. She had been sitting on her largest suitcase, and now she stood, preparatory to being greeted by the plantation manager. Relief at being rescued turned her knees to a buttery texture, and at the same time, anger churned her insides into a tighter knot. She composed herself to coolness in spite of the adrenaline flow of emotion that raced through her.

The smile that she had summoned to her lips died a slow death as the manager glanced at her then walked over to one of the two local men who guarded the supplies that had been off-loaded by the cargo ship.

"Hey, man," the manager said in greeting.

"Hey, boss," one of the other men replied.

The three men started a low-pitched conversation that sounded like a combination of English with bits and pieces of other languages tossed in.

Stassney had tried to ask the two local men earlier about transportation to Raoul and Leah's house, but they had only looked at her with polite, expressionless faces. No wonder, she thought, listening to the pidgin English. Their English was as different from hers as Russian was from Latin.

Raoul's plantation manager paused in his discussion and looked over his shoulder at her. His gorgeously blue eyes moved over her figure with a glance that was saved from insolence by the laughter that danced in their depths and by a smile that played over his expressive lips.

Stassney thought his smile was gentle, and she warmed ever so slightly toward him.

"No, darn the luck," he replied in clear English to a question put to him by the talkative helper, and they laughed.

Stassney, perplexed by his rudeness, watched the ripple of muscle in his back and shoulders as he lifted a heavy box to his chest, then gave it a toss into the ute. His white shirt was almost transparent where sweat had gathered between his shoulder blades. He had a lean frame that was less than six feet tall but gave an impression of strength as he easily stowed the boxes and burlap bags in the back of his vehicle.

His hair was almost black, and the sun glinted off the neatly cut strands as if from satin.

Stassney fluffed her bangs off her forehead again and felt a return of the weariness. Abruptly sitting down on her suitcase once more, she reflected that autumn on an island only three degrees south of the equator was merely a fact of the calendar, not of reality. She wondered if the doctor had been right to encourage her to spend two months convalescing in the South Pacific.

Patiently, she waited until it was her turn to be loaded, watching the manager—what was his name? —Sean something-or-other. She hadn't paid much attention to Leah's letter telling her how to get to the island and describing the man who would meet her and bring her to the house. She wasn't interested in men at this moment in her life. They were just too much trouble with their overinflated egos and sense of self that had to be constantly propped up by a woman's worshipful attention. So much for the stronger sex, she thought scornfully.

Sean something-or-other turned at that instant and caught the disdainful grimace on her face. She tried to smile, but the result was not a success. His face hardened, and he went back to work, opening a box and sorting through its contents as if it were filled with fine china.

She stared moodily at his dark head as he bent over his task. A hard man to know, she assessed. He could at least speak to her. It wasn't that he hadn't acknowledged her presence—he hadn't totally ignored her—he just wasn't very…*welcoming* in his attitude. Well, he didn't have to be friendly, if he would only hurry and get her to Leah's home before she totally collapsed. Heavens, what she wouldn't do for a hot bath! Make that a cool bath, she amended, glancing down at her linen dress that had started out at dawn looking fresh and crisp and now looked like something from the ragbag.

Her antiperspirant had gradually given up the battle and damp circles stained the white material under her arms, between her full breasts and along her spine.

She was hardly at her best. No wonder the men had looked at her and laughed. Lifting the straight, shoulder-length hair from her neck, she waited for a cool breeze to float by, but none did. She dropped the damp mass, which was thick and unruly, re-sisting even the efforts of a beauty shop permanent to make it curl; instead, it insisted on framing her feline face, which had a broad forehead, large, alert eyes, and a small, gently contoured chin, like a cur-tain of spicy-colored silk.

Her eyes drifted along the horizon of the sea. No other land was visible, although she knew that the Solomon Islands were to the south and the Bis-marck Archipelago was to the southwest with the mainland of New Guinea just west of that. Australia wasn't all that far, either, but she still felt cut off from civilization. Maybe it hadn't been wise to come here, after all. Misgivings crowded in on her from all sides.

Her gaze was captured by Raoul's plantation manager as he spoke to the other two men in the local language. He seemed annoyed by something, and his eyes flashed to her, then along the road that stretched silently off into the thick jungle foliage to the east and disappeared from view. Her glance followed his, then came back to him.

Their eyes met and stayed, each assessing the other in a way that was as old as life itself. For one brief, eternal second, they plumbed the depths of the other. Stassney liked what she found. He was a strong man, but a gentle one, she sensed. There was laughter in him…and friendliness when he cared to show it.

Why wasn't he being nicer to her? He was certainly outgoing with the two local men. Where had Leah said he was from? France or Australia? Or was she mixing him up with Raoul who had a French father and an Australian mother? To Stassney, he looked like the men at the university whom she had most admired—educated, at home any place in the world and self-contained.

Maybe glacial would be a better term, she thought as he looked at her once again as if wondering what he was supposed to do with her. She tamped down her rising anger. Then, to her absolutely incredulous gaze, he climbed in the ute and started the engine.

She came off her seat in a single bound and ran to the end of the wooden wharf where it joined the road.

"What do you think you're doing?" she demanded furiously.

His dark eyebrows rose at her scalding tone. "Going home," he replied with no inflection whatsoever in his baritone voice.

"And you're just going to leave me here?" She put both hands on her hips and glared at him as hard as she could. Enough was enough, and she had had it with this trip, this island and this man.

He looked at her flushed face, glanced over her luggage, then toward the back of his vehicle. "Well," he drawled, "I'm rather full up, as you can see." He sounded like a reasonable man trying not to argue with an unreasonable woman.

Stassney ground her teeth together. "I suppose your precious cargo is more important that I am?" She couldn't believe this!

"I wouldn't say that." Laughter was definitely uppermost in his murmured reply.

She drew her breath in deeply, but her haughty command was interrupted by a painful rack of coughing before she could finally snap, "You are to take me to Leah's at once! And don't think I won't report this insolent manner of yours to her!" Her thick, spiky lashes lowered over her eyes in warning, and she gave him an oblique glance full of menace.

His jaw tightened at her threat. "Well, it'll just be another black mark for her to chalk up against me." His deep chuckle was wry as he obviously shrugged off his moment of anger. "Get in," he

ordered as he swung his legs out of the doorless
ute.

Stassney climbed in while the men adjusted the
supplies in order to carry her luggage. Soon her
three cases were loaded, and Sean jumped in and
started the engine with a roar. She felt a second's
alarm as he rocketed away from the pier, than relaxed as he was forced to slow down because of
the roughness of the road.

The lout, she thought inelegantly, her humor restored now that she was once more on her way
and—please God—would soon be at her destina-
tion.

"This looks rather frightening in the twilight to
a city girl like me," she remarked with determined
cheerfulness. Looking back over her shoulder, she
saw the wharf recede from sight as they drove
deeper into the jungle and were soon surrounded by
dense foliage. The hairs prickled on the back of her
neck.

"Huh," was his noncommittal answer.

"I mean, all those knifelike ridges cutting the
skyline and then, all this wild growth in these ra-
vinelike valleys...oh!" she exclaimed as the ute
swung around a sharp, potholed curve and dropped
over a ridge into another little valley. With no door
and no seat belt, Stassney felt terribly insecure in
the lurching vehicle. She clutched the edge of her
seat with one hand and the dash with the other after
tucking her purse between her legs.

"Damn," her escort muttered. He seemed to be

listening intently to something she couldn't hear over the uneven noise of the engine.

"What is it?" she asked.

He shook his head.

Her anger boiled up again, and she wanted to do something drastic to him. She remembered an expression one of her babysitters had often used: "I'm going to smack your face but good if you don't sit down and shut up," the woman would threaten, exasperated with Stassney's incessant questions as she followed her around the house. Stassney sliced a glance at the lean male animal beside her. That's what she would like to do to him, she decided, struggling against a sudden giggle at the thought.

One of the reasons she couldn't stay angry long was because her mind roamed on tangents of its own until it found the humor in a situation. Then she would be forced to laugh, sometimes ruefully, over the pure silliness of it all.

"How much farther is it?" she asked after a long silence. The trees were silhouettes against a darkening sky.

"A lot more than it should have been," he said, turning on the headlights.

"Your lights aren't very bright," she told him.

"Very astute," he mockingly commented on her observation.

Stassney studied his profile as he struggled to keep the ute on an even keel on the dirt road. It was an all-but-impossible task, and she knew she couldn't have done it. She was reminded of the strength he had displayed while loading his supplies.

She couldn't quite figure out his attitude toward her. That he was a man of purpose, she didn't doubt. He wasn't inclined to wait on others, she thought. He would pursue his own course without needing anyone else to spur him on.

Her steady in college had needed a constant stream of admiration. When he graduated the year before Stassney and moved to New York, he had promptly found someone else to keep his ego up to par. It had been a bitter blow to Stassney, who was definitely of the romantic, till-death-do-us-part school.

She shrugged off the memory. That had been four years ago, and she had learned a lot about herself since that time. Now she only wanted to finish her last research project that would earn her a master's degree in chemistry and then get a job in a research lab. Or maybe she would teach in college and work on her Ph.D. There were lots of possibilities, and she was flexible and open to whatever opportunities life presented.

With this thought firmly in mind, she lifted her chin and glanced around, spotting a flash of color on a palm tree. Probably a parrot. There were scores of the brilliantly plumed birds in these islands.

She was rewarded for her inattention by nearly falling out of the vehicle. Wildly, she grabbed at the nearest object, which happened to be her driver's thigh. The muscles under her clutching fingers felt as if they were clad in steel instead of denim. She was afraid to let go.

The speedometer needle indicated that they were only going about ten miles per hour, yet she was being tossed from side to side as well as up and down. This was ridiculous!

"Are you sure you're on the right road?" she demanded on a gasping breath. The track dipped over a sharp ridge, swung right then left into a ninety-degree curve. She saw the muscles in his arms stand out like sinewy ropes as he fought the wheel. The engine roared as he applied gas to get them up a wet, slippery hill. Even Stassney could tell the vehicle was missing strokes in its cycle as it spluttered, caught, then spluttered again.

"Damnation!" he said.

But it was too late for imprecations or prayers. The ute dropped over the rise of the hill, and the road just seemed to disappear from beneath them. The right tire fell into a rain-washed gully that led them directly toward the ditch that had opened up near the bottom of the hill.

Stassney watched in fascinated horror as they headed for certain disaster. Her legs ached from pressing together, her purse squashed between them. One hand was holding on to the dashboard while the other dug into her escort's leg in desperation.

With a mighty heave, Sean spun the wheel to the left at the same time he used the brake and the gas pedal to control their wild plunge into the water-filled gully. The ute went into a rear-end skid that enabled him to turn the front wheels. The right tire jumped over the furrow it was following, and the vehicle slewed sideways along the muddy road, finally coming to a cracking halt with all four tires firmly implanted in individual ruts.

Sean jumped out of the ute and peered under it, using a flashlight to check for damage. "Well, that does it." He straightened.

"Will we have to walk?" she asked fearfully.

"Well, of course, we'll have to walk!" he snapped. "Or maybe we'll just spread our wings and fly off into the night like a couple of bats," he added for good measure.

Stassney drew herself up stiffly. "You don't have to shout," she said primly. She was definitely going to report this brute to Leah.

"Well, I *feel* like shouting. And maybe cursing, too. And maybe kicking myself for playing the Good Samaritan when I knew better. That's what gets me—I knew better and I did it, anyway." He was plainly disgusted with himself.

Anger, so fierce that it shook her frame, flamed over Stassney. "Good Samaritan, my foot! You've been rude and hateful and noncommunicative from the moment you arrived at the pier. And now you nearly kill me with your inept driving; besides which, I think we're on the wrong road, anyway!"

Rising to her knees on the seat, she placed her hands on her hips and glared over at him where he stood by the opening that should have been a door if the dummy had had enough sense to get a ute that had doors in the first place!

"Inept driving! You stupid female, why do you think there was no one to meet you? The roads are impassable." He pivoted from her as if he couldn't bear the sight, and dug among his cartons, checking them for damage. "Look at this! Some of my chemicals got broken." And he glared at her as if it were all her fault.

She was too busy sorting out things in her mind to respond to this latest insult. Good Samaritan? No one to meet her? Roads impassable?

She latched on to this last idea as if it were a lifeline. "Why are the roads so bad?"

"We had a torrential downpour that lasted three days. The roads are a mess all over the island. And they weren't too good to start with," he added in a sarcastic afterthought.

She looked at the ridged hill behind them and the water-covered dip in front of them. The road would have been impossible to her even if it had been dry. She swallowed hard, trying not to notice the darkness that was slowly closing in on them, making the jungle appear closer and closer. There wasn't a breath of wind stirring, and the island was eerily silent.

Her question came out slowly. "Who are you, then, if you're not Sean-somebody who was supposed to pick me up?"

"Well," he drawled, "I was wondering how long it was going to take you to pick up on that

fact.'' He straightened from his inspection and
climbed back into the vehicle. A hand settled on
her hand that held the back of the seat. She was
still sitting sideways on her knees.

She watched as his hand began a slow journey
up her arm, across her shoulder and circled the base
of her neck, tightening ever so slightly. She realized
she was supposed to feel threatened. Her darkened
gaze narrowed, and she defiantly raised her eyes to
his.

The last light of evening seemed concentrated in
those blue depths, and Stassney felt herself relaxing. Confidence returned in a welcoming surge.

''You demand a ride with a strange man and
never ask his name or for any form of identification.
Isn't that rather foolish of a woman in a strange
place?'' His hand snaked behind her neck and began a slow pressure to bring her head to his. She
resisted the movement, and his hand squeezed in
warning.

Their struggle took on more elemental nuances
as each of them tried to exert power over the other.
Neither wanted to be the first to give in.

With a little toss of her head that sent her curtain
of hair into swirling motion, Stassney spoke. ''This
isn't getting us anywhere. If you're going to hurt
or ravish me, you'd better get on with it. It's getting
dark and I'm hungry. I was afraid to eat lunch after
losing all my breakfast over the side of the ship this
morning.''

He muttered a distinct curse. ''Don't you have

enough sense to be scared?'' he demanded, taken aback by her insouciance.

She reached over and patted his lean cheek. "I recognize a pussycat when I see one. You don't have the look of a lecher or a murderer.'' Her grin was impudent.

"Oh, yeah?'' was his challenged response. He brought her lips within an inch of his. His breath fanned lightly over her face, and she caught a whiff of spearmint—he had been chewing gum when he first arrived at the wharf, she remembered—plus the scent of his after-shave, which had a clean, soap-fresh fragrance.

"I like your after-shave,'' she murmured, batting her lashes at him seductively. She almost laughed at the look of chagrin that spread over his features.

"Woman, you tempt me to teach you a real lesson…except I suspect I would be the one on the learning end of the experience.'' He released her and lounged back in his seat. "Well, this verbal sparring, delightful as it is, isn't getting us home. Come on, lady, hit the road!'' He climbed out, turned on the flashlight after coming around to her side, and helped her out of the ute.

She looked up at him, deciding he was about six inches taller than her own five feet, four inches. "By the way, I'm Stassney Murdock.''

"Paul Windham,'' he said.

His name didn't tell her a thing. She didn't remember Leah ever mentioning it. Why had her friend chalked up marks against him? she wondered as she followed him along the road. Why hadn't Leah told her something about him? Her married friend was always telling Stassney in her letters that she had an eligible man ready for her when she came to visit. This one looked very available to her.

He had nothing about him of the air of a *taken* male. No woman had ever claimed his attention long enough to lead him to the altar, she was willing to bet. He was more interested in his precious chemicals. Chemicals! This was sounding better and better.

She would have liked to ask him several questions, but it was all she could do to keep up with his long stride. Her lungs ached as they forced air in and out at an accelerated pace. A cough pushed its way past her parted lips, and she had to stop for a minute. Her escort took no notice but walked swiftly on. She could feel her anger returning.

He was much too upsetting to her equilibrium, she realized. She had never had such trouble hanging on to her temper before in her life. Of course, she was extremely tired, she thought as she lagged farther behind. She had better keep up. Soon it would be completely dark, and he would be hollering at her for the delay.

The mud on the dirt track clung to her sandals like some kind of doughy leech, oozing up over her soles to engulf her toes in a squishy embrace. It was an awful sensation to her at the moment, although at another time and in other circumstances, she had been known to enjoy stomping through mud in bare feet.

"Wait up," she finally had to call out.

Paul Windham stopped and turned toward her. "Come on," he said irritably. He hadn't been going fast but had deliberately slowed his normal pace to one he thought she could handle. It was going to be another hour before they got to his place as it was.

Stassney panted to a halt beside him. "You, sir, are no gentleman," she scolded, trying for a light tone.

"What the hell does that mean?" he demanded.

"Just that...oh, never mind." She marched past him.

Naturally, he had to take the lead again, and she furiously scrutinized his muscular back. Once more, she found herself falling behind the pace he was setting. She wouldn't call out again if she got lost in the jungle and was eaten by pygmies, she vowed.

Goosebumps speared her neck as she remembered that cannibalism was still practiced in these parts. It had been outlawed by the government, but not all the tribes might have gotten the word. Besides, most of them didn't read. She looked around nervously. It seemed a thousand eyes blinked at her from the jungle darkness.

Paul and the safety circle of the flashlight were rapidly disappearing over the hill in front of her. She speeded up.

The strap on her right sandal broke, and her foot

went one way while the shoe sank into the ooze. Stassney fell to her knees. She lost her purse. Feeling around with both hands, she encountered several objects—stick and stones—but no purse. Lord, it held her passport, identification and all her money! Desperately, she thrashed around in a widening area until she reached the side of the road.

The track sloped into another ditch at the edge, and she wondered if her things were sinking to the bottom of it. Cautiously, she searched over the edge and into the water. She tried not to think of crawly things.

A muffled snort told her there were more than snakes and such to worry about. She straightened as slowly, as she dared. Her heart thundered in her chest. She didn't breathe.

"What are you doing *now?*" an exasperated male voice wanted to know.

The flashlight played over her; then, at another snort from the ditch, swept over to it.

"Aaaaiiii," she screamed, scrambling to her feet. "An alligator!" she cried.

"Actually, it's a crocodile," Paul corrected, obviously enjoying her fright. "It's one of the harmless ones." He turned the light from the hissing reptile, which glided away on the dark water, back to Stassney. "My God, what a mess!" he said.

As the light played over her, she saw that her dress and stockings were totally ruined, her shoe and purse were lost, and mud covered her like a modernistic painting by a mad artist.

She tried to think of something humorous to say, something that would break the knot of tears that was swiftly forming in her throat, but nothing came to mind. There was just nothing that could take away the too-long day, the seasickness, the worry over being left behind at a wharf that had but one building, and then this man who obviously didn't want to have to fool with her...it was too much.

Clutching one hand over her tummy, she pressed the other over her filling eyes and sobbed with weariness.

Paul Windham stood absolutely still for ten seconds while a war waged within. He didn't want to touch her. But what could he do with a crying woman? He did the one thing a man could—he took her into his arms and held her cradled to his chest.

Chapter Two

"I'll never get home," she sobbed. "I've lost my passport and my money. They won't let me go home, and I already hate this place."

"Shh," he soothed. "We'll find your things. You can get a new passport. Mine was stolen the first night I ever spent abroad," he said, chuckling as he remembered.

"What did you do?" she asked, looking up at him. Her face was as woebegone as a lost child's.

It was a long moment before he answered, then his voice was deliberately light. "I went over to the American Embassy."

Tears clouded her eyes and rushed over her cheeks again. "There's no embassy here," she wept.

"Hey, now, stop that. Let's look around before sinking in the pits."

With an arm around her shoulders, he turned them about and shone the flashlight over the area. Her purse, barely discernible, was lying in a small hole in the road. Stassney grabbed it up and hugged it to her chest, depositing a patch of mud there to go with the ones lining the skirt of her dress. She sobbed anew.

Paul shook his head slightly, but his touch was gentle as he headed them down the track once more. He kept his arm around her, his hand resting naturally in the soft indentation of her waist. Their pace was very slow now as he sensed her exhaustion. Remembering her coughing spells, he wondered if she had the flu or bronchitis. Gradually, he became aware of the warmth of her, something he hadn't known in a long time, the soft, yielding warmth of a woman.

And she was very definitely a woman. Her breasts, full and firm, lingered in his memory from the brief interval when he had held and comforted her. Her skin had the winter paleness he associated with people from the northern United States, and her hair was full of brown and red tones with glints of sunshine trapped in them.

She was ginger, he decided on a sudden whimsical thought. Some women were vanilla; others were rosemary or pepper or cinnamon; this one was ginger—hot and spicy.

As a boy, his favorite cookie had been gingersnaps. When his mother had made them for him, he had wanted to gobble them down all at once.

His glance dropped to the woman tucked against his side, and his body responded with an aching lurch of need, surprising him with its intensity. His mouth set in grim lines.

"What about your things?" she asked. She had been so concerned with finding her purse that she had forgotten his supplies, which were probably quite valuable. Not to mention extremely difficult to come by in this part of the world, she added, frowning. "Will anyone bother them?"

She's changeable, he thought. Her moods shift like desert sands. No, that wasn't it. She showed flashes of temper, but she quickly returned to an even keel. She had sunk into despair for a few minutes, but then she had righted herself again. Now she was worried about his stuff.

"Well, some of the local population will probably go through it if they come across the ute before I can get back to it tomorrow, but they won't take anything."

"Oh, good," she said, evidently relieved at this news. She was breathing harder as the trail climbed upward. She realized they were going westward, which was sideways to their earlier route, which had been mostly to the north, discounting the zigzagging of the road. "Are we nearly there?" She hated to ask, for she had already done so several times and probably sounded like a spoiled kid to the man who tried to pace himself to her speed, but she was rapidly coming to the end of her endurance.

If they didn't reach Leah's place soon, he would have to leave her or carry her.

"Yes," he muttered. They still had a twenty-minute walk up the side of the mountain before they reached the clearing where his hut sat on the edge of a precipice. Her steps, were slowing more and more. He had to distract her. "Have you ever heard of the Cargo Cult?" he asked in casual conversational tones.

She shook her head. As she stepped on a sharp rock it occurred to her that it was rather ridiculous to have one shoe on and one off. She hadn't even looked for the lost sandal, she had been so glad to find her purse and get started toward Leah's once more. Besides, the strap was broken, she thought rather illogically.

"Well, the natives from the nearby villages always send someone down to check out the cargo when a ship puts in. Someday, they think, the supplies will be theirs."

"Theirs?" she questioned.

"Yes, they've noticed the ships come in and bring things to the white man and they think this is the source of his wealth and power. So, although it hasn't happened yet, they come down to see if their ship has come in yet."

She giggled, delighted with the story. "Like *The Merchant of Venice*." Her face went somber. "But it's sad, too. His ship did come in, but theirs won't." She looked up at him anxiously.

"Yes," he agreed. "Some tribes nearly starved

themselves out of existence at one time, I understand, and occasionally, someone has a dream and thinks it means the time has come. A few people always are ready to believe the dreamer, and they flock to the pier to wait, until reality sets in again.''

"Then do they go back to their farms or whatever their lives really are?" she asked.

"Yes," he said, "to what they really are." He spoke more as if speaking to himself, as if the words were a reminder of his own life. She glanced up at him curiously.

The flashlight cast enough light so that she could see his face in outline. Its bone structure was rather narrow with angular lines to his jaws and cheeks. The cheekbones slashed upward over the hollows of his face, while his jaw followed a parallel line below. A compassionate face, she thought. One a person could depend on.

"Is it much father?" she asked before she could stop herself.

"No, we're there," he said as they stepped into a small clearing.

The house was built on stilts like others she had seen in the islands. It had split bamboo sides and a thatched roof.

"This isn't Leah's house," she said, disappointed to the point of fresh tears. She simply couldn't go another step.

He, too, stopped. "It's mine," he said gruffly. "It's not a mansion, I admit, but it suffices."

Looking at the place through her eyes, he saw

just how primitive it was. His jaw clenched stubbornly. It wasn't all that bad. He defended his choice of home silently to the female who stared at it with hopelessness in every line of her small body.

"I can't go on," she whispered. "Please, can't I stay just for tonight?" Her voice quivered.

Paul felt like a fool. She was worried that he was going to make her keep on, when any idiot could see she was exhausted. And ill, he added as she coughed again. "Of course you can stay. Come on." He put his arm around her again and led her to the steps, practically pushing her up them.

They were built like a ship's stairs, she noted, narrow and steep, and with a rope banister to hold on to. At last, she reached the top and stood on the railed veranda until Paul went in front and opened a door for her. They went inside.

He laid the flashlight on a table while he lit a camping lantern. Finishing his task, he hung the lantern on a hook suspended from the ceiling and turned to her. Her eyes looked huge as she glanced all around. "This is your home?" she asked.

"Yes."

The single word was a challenge. She shook her head, as if refusing it. "Where do I sleep?"

A flush spread over his hard features. "Through here." He guided her into the bedroom, which contained a bed and a wicker bureau to hold his clothes. Shirts and pants hung from nails along one wall.

"I...this is your room," she protested.

"It's the only bedroom. Don't worry, I won't bother you." His cool glance swept over her.

She looked down at the mud. "I don't blame you," she suddenly joked, throwing him off balance. "I doubt if even a cannibal would find me appetizing at present." She pushed a strand of hair off her face. "If I could wash up…"

"Sit on the bed. I'll get a pan of water." He kicked off his shoes and socks in a corner and hurried out.

Stassney heard him in the other room as he poured water into a container. She sat on the bed after dropping her purse on the bureau. Carefully, she laid her dirty hands in her lap. The sheets looked clean. She closed her eyes for a minute.

Paul returned and placed the enamel basin on the floor. He took one look at the young woman sitting so still on his bed and realized she was asleep. After soaping up a washrag, he wiped her face, then her hands and arms.

"Stand up," he ordered softly, and she did.

Reaching behind her, he unzipped her dress and let it slide down her until it landed on the floor. He moved his hands under her slip until he found the waistband of her pantyhose. He slipped them down to her feet. "Sit," he said.

Stassney, drifting in a state of semiconsciousness, did as she was told. Paul removed her dress and hose from his way and proceeded to wash her knees, calves and feet after taking off her shoe. He looked fierce all at once. She hadn't told him she had only one shoe.

On the bottom of her foot, he found a deep cut. He cursed softly and went into the other room for the first aid kit. "This will burn," he murmured when he returned with the iodine.

Stassney's eyes flew open at the stinging pain, and tears filled them before she could blink them away. She stared down at Paul. He knelt at her feet, one foot in his hand while he administered the antiseptic. He blew gently on the smarting wound when he finished.

Raising his eyes, he gazed into her pain-filled ones and knew regret that he had had to hurt her. "I'm sorry," he said. "Get under the sheet now. You can sleep."

She followed his orders, her eyes closing on a weary sigh. They fluttered open. "Where will you sleep?"

"I don't know," he admitted. "I'll make a pallet."

"You can sleep on the other side of the bed," she offered graciously. Her eyes closed again, and she sank into darkness.

Paul took the dirty water and threw it out a handy window. He hung the washrag to dry on a pole when he carried the pan, which was his bathtub, his dishpan and anything else he needed it for, back into the main room. He sat in a straight chair, deep in thought for several minutes, then he turned out the lamp and went into the bedroom. Slipping out of his shirt and pants, he pulled on a pair of khaki walking shorts and, lifting the edge of the sheet, slid into bed.

His mind went over the same ground he had covered during the time he had sat in the other room. Who was she? A friend of Leah's, that much was obvious. Yes, but different from the usual women Leah had visit her. This one was no rich bitch, out for a summer fling or husband number three.

Yet, her dress was a designer model—he had noticed that when he stripped it from her. She just seemed different, he thought. Because she was ill right now. That made her seem soft and vulnerable instead of hard as nails, as most of the women he had met in the islands were. The rich friends that Leah tried to pair him with turned him off. That wasn't his scene nor his way of life. He had a job he liked, doing the kinds of things he was interested in. He had never met a woman who could live it with him, although there had been several who had tried to change it for him.

But that's not going to happen, he raged silently, as if faced with a direct challenge. The slumbering figure next to him shifted, her arm moving so that her hand rested against his side. He inched away from the contact, feeling a small jolt run through his body even as he quelled it.

It didn't seem to bother her to sleep with a man...and a stranger, too. His face felt tight and strained. He forced himself to relax. It made no difference to him if she slept with every Tom, Dick and Harry who came along. She probably did, he told himself cynically. On this note, he fell asleep at last.

At noon, with the help of several Papuans from the village, Paul got the ute up the mountain and into the clearing. It hadn't been running right for a long time, but the spare parts and various kits he had ordered had arrived with yesterday's cargo and he could now get busy fixing the engine. But first, he climbed into the hut.

Stassney Murdock was still blissfully asleep.

He stood in the bedroom doorway, frowning and unsure what to do about her. He had tried to reach the plantation by radio, the only means of communication—unless you knew how to raise anyone. Their unit must be out—a common enough problem here in the islands. Sighing, he went over and pulled the sheet back over her.

She promptly pushed it away from her. He grinned; then, without realizing he was going to do it, he leaned down and kissed her gently on her brow. Surprised, then angry with himself, he went out, ate a sandwich made from canned meat and started working on the four-wheel drive vehicle, which had started out as a Landrover, but had lost various parts in its hard life, ending up as a conglomeration of make-fit pieces.

By ten that night, Paul was pacing the length of the veranda. Stassney was still asleep. He had even taken her pulse and laid his head on her chest to listen to her heartbeat. Still, she slept.

It was damned unnerving, he thought, stopping by the open door and listening intently. Not a sound out of her. And damned inconsiderate, too. He would have to share his bed with her another night. And there was still no answer from the Laroche plantation.

He rummaged through a basket and found some cigarettes which were long, thin and wrapped with brown paper. He lit one up, although he rarely smoked and then only after a good dinner followed by a fine brandy. He paced and puffed, puffed and paced. Midnight came.

"By damn, this is too much," he gritted angrily.

Stalking into his bedroom, he leaned over Stassney, intending to shake her. She had slept nearly twenty-seven hours! Before he touched her, she sprang up in bed, her eyes wide and staring. Her movement startled him and he jerked back.

"We've got to get out!" she cried, leaping to the floor. "Oh," she said, looking at the hut, then at her host. "I'm sorry, I thought there was a fire." She sniffed delicately, sampling the air.

"I was smoking earlier," he said, again on the defensive. It was uncanny, the way she made him react, as if he were always in the wrong over something.

"I see," she said slowly. She looked at her slip and bare feet. Her gaze went to the window, which had mosquito netting drawn across it. "What time is it?"

"Midnight."

She felt rested after her brief sleep. A grin spread over her face. "Sorry I conked out on you," she apologized. "And thanks for cleaning me up."

He shrugged that aside. They stood there in a brief, awkward silence.

"Well, if I could have my dress back, or if you would lend me a shirt, I need to use the..." She stopped abruptly, realizing he probably had no bathroom.

"Through there." He pointed toward a small door at the back of the dimly lit room. He retraced his steps into the main room and out onto the porch again.

Stassney found the portable john in a tiny back room just large enough for one person. Coming back into the bedroom, she grabbed a shirt and slipped it on, then padded out into the main room.

Paul came in and closed the mosquito netting behind him. "Are you hungry?" he asked, slicing her a quick glance then looking away. He wondered if she realized just how sexy she was, standing there in one of his old shirts with bare feet and a sleepy, tousled look—as if she had just spent a couple of hours making love.

"I'm starved," she said, realizing it was true. "I haven't had anything since breakfast, and I lost that overboard." She shook her head ruefully. She went to a chair and sat down.

"That was yesterday," he said, getting out bread from a metal container and opening a can of meat. He hesitated, then opened some canned sliced tomatoes and a can of peaches. He put the containers on the wooden table with a spoon in each. He placed a plastic plate before her and laid a fork on it. He set the bread and meat out for her and got a plate and fork for himself. "Water or beer?" he checked with her. He looked into her incredulous eyes.

"Yesterday?"

He nodded. "You slept twenty-seven hours. I was pacing the floor, wondering what to do." He grinned at her.

Her hand fumbled with the neck of his shirt that she wore. "I thought it had only been three or four hours." Her voice was husky. "I slept all day?" She couldn't believe it.

"Yes." He opened two bottles of water for them.

"Where did you sleep?"

"With you. You said it would be okay, remember?"

She raised her eyes to his and saw that he was teasing her. The smile played in his beautiful blue eyes. "You have the most gorgeous eyes. It makes me jealous."

"And you," he countered, "are one of the sexiest women I've ever met. And a very nice bed-partner, too."

They grinned at each other, and both knew it was

going to be all right. They had gotten past the trou-
blesome beginning.

"Leah must be worried," Stassney began; then
she saw the radio. "Did you contact her?"

"I tried, but their unit doesn't seem to be working. I couldn't get a response." He sliced meat and
put it on a piece of bread. "Here. Eat. I thought I
would take you up tomorrow. Midnight doesn't
seem the correct time."

She absently picked up the sandwich, her mind
on other thoughts rather than hunger. "How will
we get there? Is it far?" She looked despondent,
thinking of another long, difficult walk.

He threw back his head and laughed. "You're
worse than a kid with that question. Don't worry.
"This will be an easy trip. The rover will make it
in about an hour."

"The rover?" She bit into her sandwich, decided
she liked it and ate rapidly. She helped herself to
the vegetable and fruit.

"The ute. I got it fixed today. The spare parts
finally came in. The Papuans thought I was one of
the Cargo Cult there for a while because I've gone
to the wharf every day for two months." He started
on his meal.

"The Cargo Cult," she mused, remembering the
trip up the rough road and his talking that had
helped keep her going. She remembered his arms
around her, comforting her when she felt that all
was lost. Tears touched her eyes again for some
mysterious reason.

"Hey," he called gently, "are you all right?"

"Sorry, guess I'm still a little tired. I've been...under the weather lately."

"I wondered about that." His statement invited her to talk about it, if she wanted to.

"I was caught in a fire and inhaled some smoke," she elaborated casually as if it had been a minor thing, as if her life and that of the unconscious woman's hadn't depended on her making it out the rear exit of the dress shop.

"That explains your reaction to the cigarette smoke when I went in to wake you," he said thoughtfully. "And the coughing spells." A look of remorse flickered over his face. "I owe you an apology."

"Why?" she asked, one brow going up in surprise.

"I wasn't very patient with you on the road. Or very nice to you down at the wharf."

"Oh, well." She waved his apology aside. "After all, I wasn't your responsibility. I thought you were Leah's manager. She said in her letter that he would pick me up, and the men there called you 'boss,' so I put two and two together and came up with the wrong answer."

Paul sliced the rest of the meat, dividing it evenly between two sandwiches, and put one of them on her plate. "We have to eat this, or it will spoil. I don't have a refrigerator at this house."

"Do you have one at another house?" she asked.

"Yes." He paused, but at her expectant glance,

went on, "I have a home base plus a couple of huts like this one that I work out of."

"What do you do?"

"I'm an agronomist. Do you know what that is?"

"Ummm, something to do with farming."

"Right. I study the land, helping the farmers decide what will grow best and advising them on how to do it. Right now, in addition to that, I'm working on some experimental crops that I don't know much about myself, but I want to see if they will grow in this area."

"How interesting," she exclaimed, her expressive face indicating her sincerity. "What are you growing?"

Paul glanced at his watch. "It's after one o'clock in the morning. Can we postpone this discussion until dawn?" he teased her about her eager response.

"Of course," she at once agreed, finishing her second sandwich.

They polished off the cans of tomatoes and peaches and drank down the sterile water. Stassney helped Paul clear the table and clean the dishes.

"Your suitcases are over there," he pointed out. "Use this water in the pitcher to brush your teeth but don't swallow any of it. Spit it into the basin and leave it. I'll empty it when I get through. Out the window," he said, anticipating the question he could see forming on her lips.

"Neat disposal system you have there," she commented, not sure that she approved.

"I only toss out water. Everything else I either eat, or it goes out in the ute with me when I go."

"Good." she definitely approved of that. She found her toothbrush and completed her preparations for bed. "It seems odd to be going back to bed after just getting out, but strangely, I do feel sleepy." She padded into the other room and brushed off her bare feet before lying down again. She kept the shirt on.

Paul brushed his teeth, raised the netting and tossed the used water out the window, then carefully replaced the mosquito barrier. "Are you taking malaria tablets?"

"Not yet, but I brought some with me."

He shook two out of his supply and brought one to her, giving her a fresh bottle of water to drink from. He took his pill and then drank from the same bottle. Disposing of that, he turned out the hanging lantern and came to bed. He wondered how long it would take him to get to sleep tonight.

They lay in the dark, each aware of the other, each trying not to breathe loudly, not to move around, not to call the attention of the other. It was impossible.

"It's a lot harder falling asleep tonight than last night," he finally said in a soft voice.

"Yes." She didn't pretend to misunderstand.

"I don't suppose…" he began on a hopeful note.

"No, of course not." His sigh was exaggerated.

She giggled. "I really don't know you well enough...even if you do have blue eyes that melt my insides everytime I look at you." Actually, she hadn't known any man *that* well. Her boyfriend in high school had been older and gotten drafted before events got too serious between them; the one from college had made so many demands that she had refused the final one.

Her try at humor didn't lessen the tension between them.

"Maybe I should fix a pallet in the other room," he said after another long silence.

"No, that shouldn't be necessary. We're two adults..."

"I think that's the problem, two adults alone on a tropical island together."

"...and we should be able to handle this. How about a ten-mile jog?" she suggested.

"In the jungle at night? Are you crazy?"

"So it was a bad idea. How are you at rummy?"

"Lousy."

"You play my kind of game," she told him. "Five hundred out?"

"Forget it. I'm not playing cards at this hour of the night, uh, morning." He turned toward her, his body lying alongside hers in the narrow bed. His hand touched her abdomen, found her hand resting there and took it in his. "You were so exhausted last night you wouldn't have been disturbed by an earthquake," he murmured near her ear.

"Do you have many of those?" she asked, pretending interest.

"No, just an occasional volcano eruption."

"Really?"

"What do you think caused these mountains in the islands?" he asked, his breath fanning over her neck as he moved closer.

He felt as if a volcano were going to erupt within himself at any moment. And what was he doing snuggling up to her like this? he demanded. Kissing her, came the answer. And he did.

Stassney accepted the soft pressure of his lips on hers without a smidgen of maidenly protest. She simply let herself enjoy it, knowing that it would go no farther than a kiss. When he raised his head, she said, "Your lips are as melting as your eyes."

He was irritated by her remark. He wanted her to be less composed after his kiss, he realized. She hadn't repulsed him; she had even responded, but in a way that stopped the caress on the level that it had begun. He was drawn to the challenge she presented. After an inner struggle, he forced himself to move away from her enticing form. "Good night, Stassney," he muttered several heartbeats later.

"Good night, Paul."

"And good night, America," he said, his voice wry with laughter that was directed at himself.

In the dark, Stassney grinned. A man in control of his emotions and his libido, she thought. A man of gentleness and humor and strength. A man with melting blue eyes and devastating lips. Just the type of man she had always dreamed of.

Chapter Three

Stassney woke early. She was wonderfully rested...for the first time in ages, she thought. The warmth all along her back was Paul's body, cupped into hers as if they had been fitted for each other. His arm was across her waist.

She simply lay there, savoring the sensations induced by the intimate contact. Her awareness of him grew like the brightening of the sky with the dawn. She could feel his chest move against her back with each breath he drew, feel the warm air leave his lips as he exhaled near her shoulder. Somehow it was comforting, knowing he slept so peacefully with her. A sign of trust, she thought.

At some time she became aware that he was different. He was no longer asleep. She moved, turning onto her back, and he lifted his arm, settling it back across her when she stilled. They looked into each other's eyes, the same probing, in-depth study of the day before…no, the day before that, Wednesday. Today had to be Friday.

"I've been with you for two days," she murmured in a sort of bewildered wonder.

"Yes," he said. His arm slowly withdrew until his hand rested on her abdomen. Then his fingers began a pattern of kneading.

His eyes were dark in the dim interior of the hut, the pupils dilated to capture all the available light. She thought she would lose herself in them. She wanted to, she realized.

Paul sensed her attraction as a gossamer thread stretching around him, binding him to her, to her softness, her gentle nature. It was like getting caught in a web, and no matter how much he pulled and brushed at it, he couldn't get rid of the invisible strands.

"I knew I should have left you on that wharf," he said.

Hurt flashed into her eyes. "Would you have? You started to leave."

"No, I couldn't have driven off." He denied the accusation in her words.

"But you wanted to."

"Yes."

Their eyes met, held.

"It's powerful, isn't it?" he whispered, the struggle plain in the frown etching his forehead.

"What?" A smile tugged at her mouth.

"As if you didn't know," he chided. His smile

met hers as he raised himself on his elbow and leaned over her.

"Tender, loving care from a man is a strong aphrodisiac to a woman. If more men realized that, divorce would become a forgotten legality."

He studied her expression carefully. "Is that what you feel?—gratitude?"

She shook her head. His caressing hand spread heat throughout her body, and tiny tremors, like a beginning volcanic eruption, warned her not to stay in this place. "It's much more basic than that. Deeper and on a more primitive level." She tried to explain her feelings to herself as well as him.

"Yes," he agreed. Then, "Stassney," softly, as if her name were in his thoughts and spoken against his will.

Slowly, he moved toward her waiting lips, which were parting to receive his kiss. It was inevitable, like the coming of dawn, like the falling of rain, like life, he thought.

The gentle pressure of his mouth on hers caused an escalation of the trembling inside her, and Paul, perceptive to her needs, slipped his arms around her, gathering her to his chest, partially covering her body in a protective manner. His lips, playful, serious, tender, hard, moved over hers until she wanted more.

She raised her arms, joining them more closely as she encircled his broad shoulders with a tightening embrace. She felt his tongue explore her lips, then she opened her mouth to him as he searched deeper. She was swept up into a lava flow of desire.

"How strange to come all this way and find this," she said when he released her mouth and planted a line of burning kisses along her throat.

"Is it? Is it really so strange?" He lifted his head and gazed into her eyes. "Your eyes are so beautiful. They capture me with their gentleness; they're full of endless promises."

His words added to the flames that licked so sweetly against her heated skin. "So are yours," she breathed.

He smiled slightly, and his lips returned to her waiting ones, taking countless kisses while his hand caressed up and down her side, never quite touching her breast, but making her achingly aware that she wanted to be touched.

"You're incredibly sexy in the morning. Are you always like this?" He tortured a bit of smooth flesh behind her ear.

"I don't know," she confessed. Her hands roamed restlessly along his shoulders, following the lines of muscles that were taut as he held himself off her so she wouldn't have to take his full weight.

"No?" he questioned her answer.

His hand moved to the buttons of the shirt she wore. She made no protest as he quickly unfastened each one then pushed the material aside. Her breasts rose in fitful breaths above the pristine lace of her slip.

"I've never been kissed before breakfast," she

explained with a little laugh. The mood could definitely stand lightening, she thought, fighting the vortex of desire that was drawing them irresistibly into its depths. "Until now."

Now his lips were tantalizing the space where her slip met in a vee over the sloping curve between her breasts. Her attention was suddenly riveted on his increasing male passion as his body pressed urgently against hers. Where was she letting this go? And why?

"Paul?" The word was lost as his lips closed over hers once again, and his tongue began a gentle voyage inside her mouth. She was momentarily lost to reason as stunning sensation poured all the way down her body. She had never been so aware of a man's touch and of her own reactions.

She had viewed passion with a clinical interest, knowing that she could be stirred by a man's kisses and caresses, but she had never before wanted to block out all thought and only *feel*. She could stay in this man's arms forever.

When his hand moved to her hip, sliding beneath the slip and shirt she wore, she realized that neither of them would be content with only kisses very much longer. She turned her head, breaking the increasingly passionate kiss.

"Unless you want to help raise a child, we'd better call it quits while we can." She was amazed that she could think at all. She felt so dizzy. But she chose her words with care, letting him know that she was as caught up in their embrace as he was.

It seemed an eon before he stopped his biting caresses along her neck. Slowly, he raised his head to once again gaze down at her. His eyes cleared, and he looked as if he had just returned from a far place.

"Aren't you on the pill?" he asked, his voice still husky from desire.

"No."

His face darkened in a scowl. "Why not?"

He was so obviously disappointed that she had to smile a bit. After all, it was a compliment to her femininity to be so greatly wanted. "I've never had reason to." She would have resented his questions had they come from anyone else, but she wanted him to know her, to understand her life before she met him. As she wanted to know and understand his. She grinned impudently up at him. "Your hand is on my leg," she reminded him.

His fingers tightened deliberately on the flesh of her thigh. Then, with a sigh, he released her and sat up on the side of the bed. "I knew it was too good to be true."

"Yes, well, most things in life are," she said briskly, getting up on her side of the bed and yawning widely. "What's for breakfast?"

"Me?" he suggested, opening his arms to her.

Stassney was startled until she noticed the devilish twinkle in his blue eyes. She wrinkled her nose at him. "You're okay for a quick snack, but let's have the main course."

He stood, walked around the bed and stopped beside her. "I thought that was you," he murmured seductively. At her warning look, he shrugged and turned away. "I'll bring you a pan of water to wash up in." He went out.

Later, when Stassney sat down to a meal of pan-fried toast and jelly and instant coffee, she felt much more her usual self. Clean, dressed in slacks and tennis shoes and a jungle-print blouse, she was once again in control of her emotions—and her libido, she added to herself, realizing that her sex drive was stronger than she had ever imagined it could be.

Or maybe it took a certain type of man to find the key to her passion, she mused, glancing over at Paul as he wolfed down a third slice of bread. He was handsome in a way that appealed to her enormously. She dropped her head to hide a secret smile. That was certainly an understatement. There were many aspects of him that appealed to her.

He was intelligent, educated to a degree close to her own, kind—in his own way—and capable on many levels. He had a sense of humor that he used in a considerate manner.

"What are you grinning about, brown eyes?" he said, interrupting her growing list of his admirable attributes.

She waved her hand around. "Us. This hut. The circumstances that brought us together."

"Fate," he said. His face hardened. "Don't get any ideas."

"What does that mean?" She was taken aback by his sudden harshness.

"There's no place in my life for...attachments."

She glanced all around herself elaborately. "I didn't realize I came with strings," she murmured wickedly, taunting him for his arrogance. Her laughing eyes were a dare. "Did you ever hear that one 'aww, shoot' wipes out ten 'atta boys'?"

"That wasn't quite the way I heard the expression," he said, chuckling at her censoring of the four-letter word. "But what has that got to do with our discussion?"

"Well, I was just sitting here thinking what a nice person you are, taking me in, sharing your bed and food, caring for me; then you wiped it all out with that nasty crack about attachments." She raised one haughty brow. "Naturally, I don't think you've got me forever for saving my life, so to speak."

The smile slowly left his face as he retreated into thought. Finally, he stirred. "You may be wrong. When I saw you down on the dock, looking so cool and collected as you sat there waiting, I knew you were dangerous. Then, when you leaped up when I started the engine and demanded to know what I was doing, I wanted to kiss you right then and there."

Stassney gasped at this assertion. "I never would have guessed."

The angular lines of his face seemed to grow harder. "No, not if I had had enough sense to drive on."

"But, where would I have stayed?"

"There's straw mattresses in the warehouse just for that purpose, in case someone gets stranded before their people can get down to pick them up."

Anger spread through Stassney, tightening her nerves into hard knots. "You would have left me on my own?"

"I didn't, did I?" He almost snarled.

"No, but I think you would have if I hadn't ordered you to take me with you...to Leah's." Her chest swelled with indignation as she recalled the events of two days ago.

He glared at her. "I would not."

"You wanted to. You admitted that much when we first woke up this morning." She glared right back.

"Right. Because I knew where it could lead...and did. Now I know how you feel in my arms, and I want you there again." His eyes glanced down at her breasts. He lifted a hand, cupping the palm slightly, his eyes measuring. "A perfect fit," he said.

"Don't," she protested, her breasts contracting with remembered desire at his words.

"Oh, yes, Stassney Murdock, I think I have you for life," he muttered softly.

She was shaken by this confession and by the intensity of his gaze as he refused to let her look away. Finally, she broke the contact and managed a feeble quip. "Sounds like a terminal case of lust at first sight."

"Huh! worse than that," he said, falling in with her mood. He stood. "Ready to go?"

He made her sit in the ute while he loaded it and then closed up the cabin.

"You're not coming back here?" she asked.

"Not for a while," he grunted, pulling a securing rope tight over several boxes of supplies. He climbed in and started the motor, listening for several seconds before he put it in gear and moved off down the road.

Forty minutes later, he stopped the Landrover on a jutting point of road where it rose to the crest of one of the numerous ridges they had crossed. He switched off the engine and watched her as she exclaimed over the view.

"This is really lovely," she said. "It's so…lush. Almost sinful."

The jungle spread out over the steep slopes, its growth so thick and verdant that Stassney thought she could walk on top of the vine-covered trees right down to the cliffs along the shore. Beyond the land, the ocean moved like a restless beast, constantly prowling.

Paul laughed, his humor restored during the silent drive. "Your New England background is showing."

"Yes, but, you know, I don't think a person can realize what this kind of growth is like until it's actually seen. It's so overwhelmingly alive. Even the air has a tactile quality, as if it touches you in passing." There was a sea breeze blowing today.

"It does," he told her. "The humidity stays between seventy and ninety percent most of the year. So does the temperature. Sunlight and moisture, just what every plant needs."

"Are there plantations down there that I can't see?"

"A few, not many. The land here belongs to the inhabitants, and the government is very careful about allowing sales. The large farms are used as training schools for the Papuans to learn the methods of commercial agriculture. Raoul leases his land and employs only native help," he finished on a note of approval.

She felt better at hearing this, for she had been worried about Leah's reception of Paul when they arrived. Not that her friend wouldn't be polite, but Stassney hoped Paul would be invited to the house while she was visiting, and that didn't seem likely if Leah and he had already formed a dislike for each other. But if he and Raoul were friends...

Tilting her head sideways, she gave Paul a saucy grin. "Is it very much farther to the house?" she asked sweetly.

He rolled his eyes heavenward before looking back at her. And then, the teasing laughter was gone, evaporating like a mist before the tropical sun. The grin left her face, and the mock exasperation fled from his. For long seconds, they simply stared into each other's eyes, lost in the other's depths.

"It seems a lifetime," she whispered.

"Yes," he agreed, knowing what she meant.

His hand reached out to her, cupping gently behind her neck to bring her to him. He lowered his head until his mouth touched her waiting lips.

Stassney laid a hand on his chest, experiencing his warmth and the quick beat of his heart. Her own heart throbbed painfully, and its tempestuous beat increased when he laid his free hand along her rib cage.

He spoke against her lips. "The first twenty-four hours with you were a torment because you scared me to death with your Sleeping Beauty act. The next twenty-four have driven me insane because…"

He lifted his head and stared into her eyes which glowed with slumberous flames of desire. He groaned and buried his face in her curtain of hair, his mouth tasting the honey along her neck, unable to stop.

"It hasn't been forty-eight hours," she corrected, reaching for her shield of humor, for facts, for anything to bring them back to reality.

"A lifetime." He repeated her earlier words. His lips ravaged her throat and sent chills along her arms. Just as she thought she would drown in bliss, a car came roaring along the twisting road, and they jerked apart. She caught a glimpse of blue car and a driver with flaming red hair before it shot out of sight around the bend.

"Who was that?" she asked, straightening her blouse and sitting as far from Paul as possible.

"That, I imagine, was your ride."

Stassney glanced down the tract. The sound of grinding gears could still be heard. "He drives worse than you."

"Thanks," Paul said dryly. "Now let's get you up to the house while the road is clear." He backed out and took off up the steep incline.

She settled back in her seat, holding on to the dash as usual. Her thoughts weren't on the possibility of falling out of the ute, though. The possibility of falling in love did cross her mind. And that would be very foolish, she warned herself. She was here to regain her strength after the trauma of the fire, not to get trapped in another conflagration...one that would have longer lasting and more devastating effects.

She glanced at Paul. His face was set in a determined frown, as if he were arguing with his thoughts, too. She suddenly grinned. "This is really crazy. I mean, here we are, virtually strangers, and yet, we've kissed and quarreled and slept together and...well, it's all kind of silly, isn't it?" Her gaze was anxious. "Can't we just be friends?"

His face softened at her tone. She was confused about them, but he wasn't. He knew exactly what the problem was. "I don't know if we can or not," he said truthfully. "There's already been too much between us for mere friendship. "So, I think not."

His quick smile at her softened his words, but Stassney still felt as if she had been dealt a severe blow. He didn't want to be friends with her! A flood of tears filled her throat, and she wondered at the strange phenomenon. She wasn't much disposed to tears any more than she normally was to temper, yet, here on this island, she had given in to both. Strange.

Leah, her dark curling hair flying out behind her, ran down the steps when Paul stopped in front of the house that was exactly Stassney's idea of a plantation house.

"What are you doing here?" her friend cried, hugging Stassney as soon as she hopped out of the ute. "You weren't supposed to arrive until tonight. With Raoul. Sean is going to pick you up this evening."

Stassney drew back to gaze at her friend in puzzlement. "But I told you in my letter when I would get here."

"Yes, but I left word at Port Moresby that you were to wait there for Raoul—he had to go down to Sydney on a business trip—and the roads have been impossible here for several days."

"I didn't get any message...." Stassney started to answer.

"Your radio is out," Paul interrupted. "I haven't been able to raise you for two days." He placed two of Stassney's suitcases on the steps and went back to the Landrover for the other one.

Leah looked from Stassney to Paul. "Yes, Sean has gone over to the Joliquins' place to borrow a spare part before going down to the pier later. Where did you run into Stassney?" Her gray eyes opened wide. "Where have you been for two days if you arrived on time?" Her gaze swung back to Stassney with the second question.

"At my hut over on Plantain Ridge," Paul answered for them. "I picked her up at the wharf when I went down for my supplies."

"But, why did you take her over there?" Leah obviously thought this had been the wrong decision.

Paul's face became remote. "Because I hoped I could get through to here. But I couldn't. The ute broke down, and we had to walk up the ridge. Stassney was exhausted." His blue eyes flashed to her, and his expression softened. "We'd better get her in now. And she needs a decent breakfast. We only had toast and coffee."

Leah at once became the efficient hostess. "Of course, darling, come on in." With an arm around Stassney, she led her inside the house, giving orders all the while to a team of servants who appeared as if at an unspoken command. "Will you join us?" she said, remembering Paul, who stood by the ute.

He hesitated, then nodded, following them into the house.

The floors were a shining terrazzo covered with woven grass rugs. Stassney realized that, with the house being high on a mountainous plateau, it didn't need to be built on stilts as the ones lower or deeper in the jungle did. The furniture was of a light and airy design, mostly made from rattan. Several tables had wooden frames with glass insets, so that she could see the floral arrangements on the floor beneath.

Some of the clay pots held ferns or vines, but others were filled with orchids that Stassney knew must grow in the jungle, wild and beautiful. One plant, with a tiny bloom that was pale pink, had darker spots along its petals. She thought it looked like a blushing girl who had freckles.

"Here, darling, sit down in this chair," Leah ordered, all concern for her guest.

In a few minutes, Stassney found herself eating a breakfast of bacon and eggs and croissants, finishing off the meal with a marmalade of tropical fruit. She sat back contentedly with a fresh cup of coffee and gazed out over the plantation. "This is really marvelous," she said approvingly of the view.

"We'll go for a walk, and I'll show you all around," Leah promised.

A dark scowl formed on Paul's face as he replaced his coffee cup in its saucer and wiped his mouth on the damask napkin. "She needs to rest. She was sick on the ship and then she had a long walk through the mud. She cut her foot." His stern glance went to Stassney. "Watch that cut. Keep it clean. If it opens up, be sure and use iodine on it."

"Yessir," Stassney said meekly, lowering her head, then looking at him from beneath her spiky curtain of lashes. She laughed as he looked chagrined at her obvious mocking of his orders.

"Did you two get along like this from the first?" Leah asked dryly, her tone indicating it was what she had expected. Beneath her friendliness to him was a biting edge of sarcasm.

Stassney grinned openly. "No, I yelled at him at first."

"Then she went to sleep on me," Paul continued. "I thought she must be a descendant of Rip Van Winkle."

Stassney's eyes twinkled with mischief. "And here I was thinking I must be Robinson Crusoe, cast up on a strange island and rescued by my man Friday."

Paul wasn't amused. "You slept twenty-seven hours, remember?" he said softly.

Leah looked concerned. "She just got out of the hospital the day before she left. I was afraid that was too soon."

"The hospital?" Paul snapped, turning a fierce gaze on Stassney, who flushed slightly.

"Didn't she tell you? She's a hero. She was caught in a fire in Kim's dress shop, and she single-handedly dragged out a customer who was injured. And the woman weighed fifty pounds more than Stassney."

Stassney didn't miss the quick, hard look that passed between the other two at the mention of Kim

Troussard. She wondered what it meant. Kim had visited Leah last spring, she remembered.

"Why didn't you tell me that?" Paul demanded of Stassney.

"I told you I had suffered from smoke inhalation...."

"You made it sound like nothing. How did this fire start?"

Stassney controlled her irritation. He sounded like a fire marshall, and she expected him to whip out a pad and start taking notes any moment.

"It was a new shopping mall, built in an old warehouse area, using the renovated buildings to house the new stores. The siding of weathered wood was quaint, and the wandering boardwalks with wooden stairs connecting the various levels were enchanting, but they were also a fire hazzard and difficult to find your way out of in an emergency." Stassney shrugged as if it didn't matter now. "The fire started in a fast-food restaurant and spread rapidly. This other woman and I were back in the fitting room. By the time we realized there was a fire, the front of the store was engulfed in flames."

"Where were the clerks? Weren't there other people in the store?" Paul asked in hard tones.

"Yes, but they didn't realize we couldn't hear the alarm from where we were. We had to drop out a window to a lower level...."

"And the woman hit her head and Stassney had

to help her out," Leah broke in. "They both nearly died from the smoke."

Stassney's eyes went dark as she remembered the first paralyzing wave of panic that had swept over her and the customer whose dress she was fitting. The woman had become hysterical, but some other part of Stassney had taken over her reactions. It had been driven by one compulsion—survival.

For a second, she was back in the burning complex, her eyes sweeping every level in search of escape as she first dragged, then guided, the semiconscious client along the stairs and walkways until she worked their way free of the roaring flames.

She could still hear the noise of the fire—unbelievable noise. Explosions all around her as bottles and pressurized cans became overheated, the hiss of steam and escaping gases sounding like a pit of snakes, with her and her burden right in the middle of them. She hadn't had time for fear at that moment, she realized. But now it came back to haunt her at odd times—her eyes went to Paul—such as when she caught a whiff of smoke.

A hand closed over hers, large and strong and comforting. "Don't think of it anymore," Paul said gently.

She breathed deeply, eradicating the memory. Her lungs protested and erupted into a coughing spell.

"You coughed a lot in your sleep, too," he commented thoughtfully. "I should have realized how sick you were."

"I'm not really sick. All the little hairs in my lungs are busy sweeping out the carbon particles, that's all." She indicated to a white-clad servant that she would like more coffee when he paused beside her with the silver pot, then she changed the subject from herself. "You never did tell me about your crops, or how an agronomist got to this part of the world," she reminded him.

Paul relaxed in his chair after accepting another cup of coffee for himself. "The State Department arranges things like that. I was teaching at the University of Arizona when they invited me to take part in an exchange program: one agronomist of ours for ten students of theirs," he added, sharing the private joke with Stassney.

"I'll give you one 'atta boy,'" she said, pretending to give him a point by drawing a line in midair.

Leah was annoyed at the undercurrents that she didn't understand. "What are you two talking about?"

"Stassney just gave me a point. Maybe it will offset some of the black marks I have in your book." He chuckled at the irritated moue that Leah gave him.

"I really should disown you," she muttered vengefully.

"But you like me too much," he teased.

"Raoul likes you. I merely tolerate you."

"Just don't try to do me any more favors," he told her.

Now it was Stassney who didn't understand the quips being tossed back and forth. "What are *you* two talking about?" she demanded.

Leah flashed Paul one more icy gray glance before turning to Stassney. "You remember last year when Kim visited me?"

Stassney nodded, feeling a flicker of precognition for what was coming.

"Well, it seems that when she was in college, her folks took a vacation on an Arizona dude ranch, taking her with them. Guess who was working there that summer?" Leah paused expectantly.

"Paul?" Stassney questioned faintly.

"Uh-huh. They had a mad fling, and when she saw him here and told me about it, naturally I tried to get them back together, but Mr. High-and-Mighty Windham was having none of it." She cast him a glacial look.

Color had crept across his strong cheekbones, and his lounging pose disappeared as Paul sat up straight. "We did not have a mad fling. She chased me all over the place until it was embarrassing. Then you threw her at me until I had to take to the hills to get some peace to do my work," Paul accused gruffly.

A grin worked itself onto Stassney's pink lips. She knew just how determined Kim was. That was why she was now a successful designer with several boutiques of her own. She had drive and a fierce determination to achieve whatever goal she set for herself. Had she really made Paul one of those goals?

A quick, hot jealousy flamed through her only to be followed at once by the realization that Kim hadn't succeeded this time. She studied Leah. Was her friend now flinging Stassney at this elusive male? Was this the man Leah had picked out and written her about?

Brown eyes, as dark and secretive as a jungle glen, switched over to contemplation of the man. Was Leah's obvious maneuvering the reason he had been so reluctant to get involved with her down at the wharf on Wednesday? He needn't worry. She wasn't anxious to get involved, either. She had her studies and her future to think about.

Paul was intensely aware of Stassney's scrutiny. He found himself wondering what she thought of him. She felt a physical attraction, he knew that, but gratitude for his tender, loving care as she had termed it could account in part for that.

He was startled by a plunging despair that seemed to lower his spirits by several degrees. He had recognized the K.T. label on her dress when he removed it. Kim Troussard. The same initials were on the pocket of the slacks she now wore. And she was a friend of Leah's. That could only mean one thing. Stassney was as wealthy as the other two women were.

Although she didn't seem to be spoiled by her money as the other rich women had been that he had met in this house, still she was one of them, used to having things her own way.

It was one thing to rough it for a while; it was another to live in poverty...not really poverty, he admitted truthfully, but in harsh conditions. After all, he had to go where his work took him, and that was sometimes to remote parts of the world. Like Papua New Guinea, a South Seas paradise that was still reaching for the twentieth century. A man couldn't expect a woman to live as he did, especially one who came from a rich home.

He frowned at the path his thoughts were taking. What was he doing thinking about living with a woman anyway? My God, that would be the height of stupidity, to start thinking along those lines. An impossible dream. Especially with someone like Stassney.

His life would have been difficult for a woman who was used to a modest life; to someone who had lived in the lap of luxury all her days, it would be ridiculous to ask it of her. Not that he had any intention of asking anyone to do so, of course, but if he had, it certainly wouldn't be Stassney Murdock!

Stassney was shocked at the glare Paul turned on her. He looked as if he were accusing her of some foul deed, but she hadn't an inkling of what she could have done to set him off like this. Her own anger rose to meet his, and they stared balefully at each other, totally silent.

Leah was unaware of the sudden tension.

"How's the dear old alma mater?" she asked Stassney and immediately explained to Paul. "Stassney, Kim and I went to the same preparatory school, Elizabeth J. Williamson Academy for Gifted Students. We were, of course, bright, bitchy and beautiful as all WAGS must be. Get it?...W-A-G-S, Williamson Academy for Gifted Students. We were always making puns on the name and getting punished for it. Stassney was once grounded for two weeks...."

"I was nearly expelled!" Her grin was definitely impish, widening her well-defined lips into upturned bows and inviting the other two to laugh with her.

Paul smiled at their girlish manners, understanding their mood of reminiscence. Men did the same when they got together with old friends from childhood, retelling football victories or some scary experience and laughing at their youthful excesses. He found himself fascinated with this glimpse of the young woman who had slept so trustingly in his arms for two nights.

A tightening sensation in his chest surprised him as he considered Stassney's trust in him. She seemed to have had complete faith in him from the very first moment she laid eyes on him. Why?

Because she has never been roughed up by life, he decided. He didn't begrudge her the easy existence he envisioned for her, but he thought of his own life—his struggle to get through college, working at whatever jobs he could find, sometimes having to make a choice between buying books or food, and finally, making it through the master's program—and realized anew just how different his life had been from this pampered girl's.

The smile faded from his eyes. Stassney had never been disillusioned by life. He wouldn't be the one to do it for her. She was drawn to him for some reason, and heaven knew that he was bowled over by her! But that was as far as it was going to go. No more getting mixed up with spoiled young girls. He had been through all that almost five years ago with Anne. No more!

"What did you do?" he asked, bringing himself back to the discussion of childhood pranks.

Leah answered. "We were marching into the auditorium for some special event, and the English teacher chewed us out for talking in line and also for letting our hips sway as we walked, so Stassney quipped, 'What barks at one end must wag at the other.'" Leah burst into uncontrollable giggles. "I thought…I…would die!"

Stassney assumed a droll expression. "Yes, but I nearly did." She turned to Paul. "My mother was so furious.…"

"Her mother was head mistress, and she grounded Stassney for two weeks, which made her miss the homecoming game and the dance.…"

"And I had a date with the cutest guy at the military academy in town," Stassney finished glumly. "I never did see him again."

Paul grinned perfunctorily at her exaggerated

wail, but his mind was busy sorting through the new facts. "Your mother *worked* at the school?" he asked, confused by this information. It interfered with his image of her past.

"Yes."

The brief answer told him nothing. He wanted to know why. The word was out before he could stop it. "Why?"

Stassney looked startled. "Well, to support us." As Paul continued to stare at her, she elaborated. "When my father died, we found out...that is, he was a sort of entrepreneur and he had overextended his resources, so he had borrowed on his insurance...and, anyway, my mother had to go to work. She had a degree in education, and she had taught high school English before I was born, so she got on at the academy."

"And became head of it?" Paul asked, his eyes narrow and probing.

"Well, yes, after earning advanced degrees in school management." Stassney was puzzled by his intensity.

"How old were you when your father died?"

"Nine," she said. "I was fourteen when my mother was made head mistress by the governing board," she added to forestall any more questions.

She didn't like remembering those five hard years, the struggle as her mother had counted every penny while keeping a smiling face turned to the public, the times Stassney had heard her weeping quietly at night. It was during those years that Stassney, too, had learned to smile and keep her tears inside. More than once her humor and ability to look on the bright side of life had saved her at trying moments.

"But your family was wealthy before that?" Paul continued.

A tender smile touched Stassney's face as she remembered her wonderful, flamboyant father. "We lived high on the hog," she admitted with a husky laugh. She, personally, would never marry a man like her father, one who was always taking a chance, living on the outside of a dare, but she had loved him as only a child can love. After his death in an automobile accident, she had learned that life wasn't always sunshine and lollipops, but there were other aspects to it just as important. Her gaze went to the man who sprawled comfortably in the padded rattan chair, his long, lean flanks outlined by the pull of the fabric stretched along his legs. She could remember in exact detail what his body had felt like pressed against hers.

With the memory came a shortening of her breath and a terrible longing inside, almost a pain, to be in his arms again. What was it about him that attracted her so strongly? His strength that he had made available to her when he helped her up the trail to the hut? His TLC when he got her there and realized how exhausted she was? His obvious dedication to his work? His drive and determination? He was the opposite of everything her father had been...and he was all she had ever thought she wanted in a man of her own!

Paul's eyes went from her to Leah and back. He abruptly shoved himself out of the chair. "I've got to go. Don't get up. I'll let myself out. Thanks for breakfast."

And he was gone before they hardly had time to realize it.

Chapter Four

"Excuse me," Stassney said and ran after him. She was panting by the time she reached the ute. Paul was already inside the vehicle. He waited until she stopped coughing, but his manner was impatient. "I wanted to say thank you for everything you did for me," she said when he was able to speak.

"It was nothing." His tone was repressive.

"But it was," she protested too strongly.

He shrugged, reaching for the ignition key. "Good-bye, Stassney." He heard the finality in the words and was glad. He wanted it that way. A clean break.

Stassney searched desperately for words to hold him. "You didn't show me your crops," she blurted out.

His hands clenched on the steering wheel until

the knuckles showed white. "Drop it, brown eyes," he ordered softly.

She lifted defiant eyes to his. "Why?"

Through tight lips he said, "Raoul and Leah can show you the progress on their place. You'll find it interesting."

"I don't want them to show me." She was stubborn.

"Then Sean can."

"And am I never to see you again?" she demanded lightly.

He was annoyed by her perceptiveness and by the hurt he could sense that she was hiding. "What would be the point?" he asked brutally.

She considered the question, watching him closely as she did. His drowning blue eyes were fixed at some point on the horizon, refusing to look at her. She wanted to reach out and turn his head so that he faced her. She wanted to touch him, she realized.

As if reading her thoughts, he moved his head, the breeze catching the dark strands of hair and blowing them across his forehead. His eyes locked with hers. After an eternity of longing he spoke to her. "We might find ourselves with that child you mentioned earlier. From what you said, about not taking the pill, I assume you don't sleep around."

Stassney recalled the past two nights when she had slept in his arms. Her lips quirked in a smiling challenge. "You were the first ever."

He nodded. "A virgin," he murmured as if it were some strange breed he had just discovered.

"Is that as bad as the common cold," she inquired with just the right amount of wide-eyed interest. "It isn't catching, is it?"

"Don't give me any smart talk." He was in no mood for joking. His life was being totally disrupted and she was cracking jokes! He wanted to belt her one...no, he didn't. He wanted to kiss her a thousand times. Sighing heavily, he gazed at her mouth. "You have the sexiest lips," he heard himself say. Damn!

"Thank you," she said wryly. She was having a hard time following his mood shifts. And her own, too. One minute, she was meltingly tender toward him, and the next, she was furious. Maybe the fire had affected her more than she had realized.

He leaned toward her, and her mouth shaped itself for his kiss, her lips going soft and parting slightly. He touched her gently, only with his mouth. Their kiss said several things, speaking of passion, questioning its right to existence and, finally, telling of the hopelessness of pursuing this strange attraction.

He lifted his head. "You're not the type for an affair, and I can't offer more to you, Stass." He sounded profoundly regretful as he caressed the underside of her chin with the back of one finger.

"Not even friendship?"

"I think not," he whispered slowly, withdrawing

his hand. "It would be too much of a strain, I'm afraid."

She stepped back. "Good-bye, Paul." She smiled, and it was the sweetest sight he thought he had ever seen. It brought a pain, a physical pain, into his chest.

"Bye, Stass. Hope you have a nice vacation." He started the ute and put it into gear.

"Paul! I forgot to tell you. We're having a party tomorrow night for Stassney. You're welcome to come. I'll try to protect you from man-hungry women." Leah came out of the front door and stood on the steps to issue her invitation.

"Thanks, Leah, but count me out." He looked at Stassney once more, then drove off.

Stassney watched him until he drove out of sight, her eyes gazing after him with a deep, unconscious hunger in their depths. It was just as well, she sighed to herself.

"What's going on between you two?" Leah demanded.

Stassney turned and went up the steps. "Nothing." And that was exactly the truth, no more, no less.

"Then what was that long, soul-searching look between you all about just before he left?"

Stassney shook her head slowly. "I don't know. He confuses me. And I think I do the same to him. When we met, something *clicked*, but..." She shrugged helplessly, unable to explain what she didn't understand herself. "Was he the mysterious man you wrote me about in our letters to each other? The one you had in mind for me?''

"No," Leah denied emphatically. "He's too dedicated to his work. Or maybe he's a woman-hater. I don't know. He won't admit much about himself."

"Oh?"

"I've only gotten information in bits and pieces. You already know he's an agronomist on loan to the Department of Lands and Environment. He teaches classes in agriculture at various places on the island as well as trying new crops." Leah's voice warmed with admiration.

Stassney was avidly interested, but she thought it wiser to change the subject. Paul Windham was a difficult topic for her. She grinned engagingly at her friend. "Enough about him. Now tell me all about your life here. Start with day one."

"It's been a learning experience, living here," Leah confided. "Your mother would be proud of me, I think."

"I'm sure she would," Stassney murmured. She paused at the top step and gazed back toward the thick growth beyond the well-tended yard. Where had Paul gone? Back to his house near this one? Or on down to one of the huts he occupied?

"I'll tell you about the parts I think you're most interested in," Leah promised. Laughing softly, she led Stassney along a corridor to the guest bedrooms.

Stassney followed Leah into a lovely suite complete with an alcove the size of a small room and a private bath that was sumptuous in pink and gold tones. "This is fabulous!" she exclaimed sincerely. "But where does the power come from?" She pointed to the electric lightswitch.

"We have our own hydroelectric plant. The islands have unlimited potential from all the streams running off the mountains...and the hundred-plus inches of rain each year," Leah explained. "Ridgecrest Plantation is part of a model program to train the Papuans...."

"Oh, Paul mentioned that last night, no, this morning. Stassney frowned, recalling other words that had passed between her and Paul.

Leah flung herself into a silk-covered French boudoir chair, stretching her legs along its curved length. Stassney walked around, admiring the room, before settling on the windowseat in the alcove. She gazed out over a spectacular panorama of cultivated growth as verdant as that of the wild jungle forest. Everything grows fast here, she mused. Everything.

Leah toyed with a curling strand of dark hair. Her candid gray eyes studied Stassney, who was removing her shoes preparatory to propping her feet on the quilted padding of the windowseat. "So you and Paul discussed the plantation, did you? What else did you talk about during the two days you spent with him?" This last was said with a teasing inflection. A sardonic grin curved her mouth.

Stassney laughed and shook her head, then became serious. "Actually, not very much. I slept

most of the time. You were going to tell me about
your life?'' she reminded.

''I met Paul almost a year ago. Raoul has known
him for about five years, I think, but I didn't until
he moved to Lyra. When I mentioned Paul in a
letter to Kim, she immediately began plans for a
visit. I didn't know that she had known him years
ago, before we knew her well.''

Kim was four years older than Leah and Stassney. Although they had known her at the prep
school, she hadn't become their close friend until
their last year in college. Liking her designs and
admiring her struggle to get started in spite of her
family's disapproval, Leah had urged her father to
invest, while Stassney had boldly gone to her godfather for the same purpose. Now, four years later,
those investments were paying off handsomely.
Kim Troussard Fashions, Inc. was firmly established, the K.T. label as familiar as a Dior.

Thus, Kim had been able to hire Stassney on
weekends at one of her boutiques and insisted on
supplying both her friends with her latest designs.

''Had they been in love before?'' Stassney asked,
experiencing a jab of hurt but unable to tell if it
was for Kim, Paul or herself. With sudden insight,
she knew she didn't want him to have been in love
with another woman.

Leah raised her hands palms up and let them drop
to her lap. ''Kim says yes; Paul says no. I guess
she was in love and he wasn't. I wish she had told
me the situation before she arrived. I could have

warned her that Paul had just gone through a difficult period with a divorced friend of mine who
simply *threw* herself at him. Poor dear, he did try
to be nice and yet fend her off at the same time.''
She giggled at the memory. ''But it's not my fault
that all the women take one look at those blue eyes
and that coal black hair and go ga-ga over him. He
accused me of setting him up!''

Stassney groaned silently. No wonder he hadn't
wanted to pick her up at the wharf. And then she
had forced him to let her spend the night, telling
him it was okay for him to sleep with her! Naturally, he had thought all the worst things about her
and assumed it was also okay to make love to her.
Actually, he had been awfully decent about the
whole episode considering what he had probably
gone through due to Leah's other visitors.

Heaving a deep breath of disappointment, she acknowledged that he was right not to see her again.
They were attracted to each other, and he had given
her plenty of warning that he wanted no attachments of any kind. So be it.

''How old is he?'' she asked.

''Thirty-one. Inez, the divorcée, talked me into
giving a birthday party for him while she was here.
I thought he was going to walk out after she gave
him a birthday kiss that should have been in an X-
rated movie.''

Stassney's fists clenched in a paroxysm of anger
on his behalf. The woman obviously had had no
sense of decency. Slowly, she uncurled her fingers

and forced herself to relax. As Leah talked on about life on the island and the other plantation owners she would meet at the party on Saturday night, Stassney became drowsy. She smothered several yawns before giving in. "Leah, would you be offended if I took a nap before lunch?" she asked.

"Not at all. That's what you're here for, to rest and recover. I'll call you in, um, two hours. How's that?"

"Fine. And thanks for having me," Stassney said sincerely.

Leah paused at the door. A worried look entered her eyes. "I hope you don't find yourself a victim of unrequited love," she said in gentle warning before she went out without waiting for a response.

"Me, too," Stassney murmured as she lay down on the satin spread and went to sleep.

Raoul, slender and elegant as only a Frenchman can be, was as warm and outgoing as his manager, Sean Stevenson. Both men had been born in Perth, Australia and were distantly related. Leah and Raoul had met in Paris two years ago, and it had been love at first encounter when he had spilled an icy drink down her back.

Stassney and Sean laughed themselves hoarse at the recounting of the love affair which had taken on the nature of an international intrigue as Leah sought to avoid the pursuing French-Australian and he had chased her unmercifully from Paris to New

York, then to California and back to New York before she had given in.

"He scared me," Leah said, explaining her flight. "Men can be so...so...*adamant!*"

Raoul touched her arm gently. "I was desperate."

Husband and wife smiled into each other's eyes in a look full of tender meaning, and Stassney's throat closed with the beauty of it. That's the way it should be between a man and a woman, she realized. Both wanting and giving to each other. No reluctance, no fears that their freedom would be taken from them. To each of them, a future without the other was unthinkable.

Sean moved suddenly, and her eyes flicked to him. For a second, she thought she saw something like pain in his eyes; then it was gone and he was smiling at her, an invitation on his lips. "Would you like to stroll through the shrub garden?"

"He's going to seduce you in the moonlight," Leah advised, giggling at the scowl Sean focused on her.

"Do you have to give away all my plans?" he demanded.

Stassney stood. "I'd love a moonlight stroll, but could we plan the seduction for another evening? I don't think I'm quite up to it yet."

Laughing, she accepted her escort's arm and went outside with him. He was very tall, she noted as they walked along the flagstone terrace. And handsome in a bigger-than-life way. With his height and massive shoulders, his flaming hair and blue-green eyes that rivaled Paul's startling looks, he was a vibrant specimen of prime manhood. He was also in love with Leah, she discerned. The fact seemed to form a bond between them for some reason. She felt *gentle* toward him.

"How did you end up on this island?" she asked as they walked among the several varieties of hibiscus that lined the paths of the garden. The tropical moonlight was enough to seduce the senses by itself, she noted, gazing at the large silver sphere. She imagined what it must look like shining on the sea.

His deep voice was a pleasant rumble as he spoke. "I wrote Raoul asking if he knew of anyone who needed a farmhand, and he wrote back that he did. He turned over the plantation to me and went off to the States...."

"And came back married?" she asked.

"Yes," he said. "His business dealings take him to Australia quite a bit. And to France. He has an interest in a vineyard there, and he and Leah go over a couple of times a year."

"They come to Connecticut, too. I saw her last Christmas at her family home."

They reached the end of the garden path and stood by a low stone wall. The plateau dropped off to a lower plain, and Stassney could see orderly rows of trees stretching off into the moon-silvered darkness. Without speaking, they sat on the wall and gazed out over the view. Stassney wondered if

Paul were somewhere looking at the same scene. Where was his main house?

"I see Paul is at the guesthouse," Sean said. "Raoul offered it to him to use as his headquarters. I thought he would be up for dinner tonight. He usually likes to check with me right away on the experimental crops we're growing under his direction."

"He mentioned those to me," she murmured. "Is that his house, down there where the light is shining through the trees?"

"Yes." Sean turned back to her after peering over his shoulder toward the guesthouse. "It was a piece of luck, meeting up with him. He's taught me more about land management than I learned in thirty years at my father's ranch."

She was puzzled. "Why did you leave Australia?" She realized she was prying.

"My father and I got along like a snake and a mongoose," he told her with no particular inflection in his voice.

He was a deep man who kept his feelings carefully hidden, she judged. She liked him more and more. Especially since he was so complimentary about Paul's abilities as an agronomist. She felt herself puffing up with pride.

When Sean stood, she let him take her hand and pull her up, then she tucked her hand into the crook of his elbow and they went back inside to talk to the other couple until late.

When she went to bed, Stassney found the large

room strange and empty, the silk sheets and firm mattress nonconducive to sleep. She thrashed around restlessly. Finally, she got up and slipped into a silk robe—another gift from Kim. In fact, Kim had insisted on outfitting Stassney with a complete wardrobe for this trip, a hard determination in her eyes as she brushed aside Stassney's objections.

"No man will be able to resist this," Kim had said as she designed one outfit after another for Stassney.

At the time, Stassney had thought her friend had been thinking of the mysterious man that Leah had in mind for her, but now she wasn't so sure. Leah had definitely been thinking of Sean as the perfect mate for Stassney—she had admitted as much that afternoon when they had talked—but Stassney thought Kim had been planning some kind of revenge on Paul for his rejection.

She sighed unhappily as she went out on the terrace. The light was still on down at the guesthouse. What was Paul doing? Reading up on his agricultural endeavors? Or was he thinking of her, only a quarter-mile from him? Hah! she scoffed at her own musings.

She shouldn't have come here. The doctor had been wrong to encourage it. Now she was caught up in the tangled threads of other people's lives, and it was too difficult for her right now. She longed to be back in the cool orderliness of her lab, doing her own experiments. Eight or ten weeks of concentrated effort and she would be finished with her individual research project. Then she would be free to go wherever she wanted.

Yes, she vowed firmly, that was exactly what she wanted. And that was probably what Paul wanted, too. So he could go his way and she would go hers. She went back to bed and tried to sleep. After a few minutes, a smile quirked her lips. The problem, she admitted to herself, was that she didn't believe a word she was saying. She had never met a man who touched her so thoroughly as Paul. He had captured her heart, her imagination and her soul.

A dream man. And a challenge. She wasn't the type to ignore the provocation that he represented. How long could he resist the attraction between them?

"I'm not sure you look rested," Leah commented as the two women lingered over coffee at the table on the terrace. The sky was a cloudless blue and the day promised to be another hot one.

"I wake myself up coughing," Stassney admitted. "But my lungs are getting better fast. The burning, breathless feeling is almost gone. Unless I try to do too much." She thought of the long hike up to Paul's cabin.

"Here. Read the paper." With a sparkle in her gray eyes, Leah pushed the front page section into Stassney's hands.

The name at the top proclaimed the paper to be the *Nu Gini Toktok*. Stassney quickly skimmed several lines of newsprint. "I can't read this. What language is it?"

Leah laughed delightedly. "It's pidgin. With over seven hundred tribes in the islands, each with their own dialect, the government encourages English as the common language, but pidgin is already established. If you read the words phonetically, you can figure out most of them. See, this is the *'New Guinea Talktalk,'*" she explained, pointing to the masthead.

Faced with a challenge, Stassney couldn't resist. She spent most of the morning reading the paper aloud to Leah who eagerly coached her in the new language. After lunch, she took a nap. Later, Sean drove her about the plantation in the blue car, being very careful on the rough roads. Several times they came upon work crews that were busy with repairs, smoothing the ruts and shoveling gravel into them.

"We try to keep maintenance crews as an ongoing thing," Sean explained. "The locals see no need for constant, daily labor. In some ways, the jungle makes life too easy, in others, too hard."

Stassney understood something of what he was saying. "Are there many people on this island?"

"Less than a thousand, most of them Papuans."

"I thought they were all Papuans," she said.

"There are three different basic types—Negritoes, the mountain pygmies; the Papuans, who are medium in height; and the Melanesians, who are the tall tribes who live along the coasts. Papua is a Malay word meaning frizzy hair."

They drove into a small village, stopping to watch the activities going on around them. The people apparently were used to visitors, for they went on with their work while the children crowded around asking for chewing gum, which request was easily understood by Stassney. Sean handed out several packs.

"It's the sugarless kind," he explained. "Paul got after me about the other."

His friendship and respect for the other man were obvious, and she had to forcibly subdue the surge of emotion she felt at just the sound of his name. Paul had closed the door on any kind of relationship between him and her. She must remember that.

"That's the *house tamboran*." He pointed to the largest structure after shooing the youngsters away. "The men's exclusive clubhouse."

Her brows drew together in a mock ferocious frown. "Now there's a part of this culture that needs changing."

The teasing light in his eyes reached his mouth. "Yes, well, you must admit it has its appeal."

"I don't want to hear about poor abused men and their need to get away from nagging women and squalling children. I am definitely nonsympathetic!" she declared, enjoying their battle.

Sean chuckled. "The *house tamboran* always draws a response from women visitors. Leah insisted that Raoul have a house built for the women, but the villagers thought that was crazy, so it wasn't done." His voice softened as he mentioned Leah.

Stassney found herself worrying about Sean, wondering if he realized he was in love with his cousin's wife…and if Leah or Raoul knew it. Was her own increased perception due to the turbulent feelings aroused in her by Paul? Stop thinking of him! she ordered her wandering mind.

At that moment, a man stepped out of one of the grass huts. He was dressed only in a pair of cutoffs, and the sight of his bare chest and limbs brought an ache of desire to her throat.

"There's Paul," Sean said. "Hey, Paul!"

Paul walked over to the station wagon with a lazy spring to his step. His tan skin gleamed in the afternoon sun, and the dark mat of hair on his upper torso seemed to invite her touch. Stassney deliberately looked away, letting her gaze roam where it would.

"Sean. Stassney." He said their names in greeting. "You two out for the grand tour?"

"Yes. I was just giving her a quick drive-by. Got to get back early for the corroboree tonight. Are you coming? I need to talk to you about that crop of beans."

Paul shook his head, his dark hair settling into attractive disarray around his angular face. "I'll see you tomorrow." His blue eyes turned to Stassney. "I just bought you a present. Wait a minute."

She watched in growing confusion when he loped off, going back to the hut. He returned in a short time, carrying a pair of sandals in one hand.

"Here." He thrust them at her. "To replace the one that got lost."

The shoes were sturdy leather straps fastened to soles that looked like tire treads. "Thank you," she said softly, warmed by his thoughtfulness.

"It was the least I could do after hurrying you along and not letting you find yours." He spoke brusquely, as if he were ashamed of his behavior and trying to make up for it.

Stassney felt the warmth drain out of her. "My sandal broke. That's why I lost it, not because of you." She handed the shoes back to him and looked stonily straight ahead.

Paul glanced rather awkwardly at the sandals he now held again. He laid them in her lap. "Well, I have no use for them," he said defensively. She was one difficult female to deal with, he thought angrily. He suddenly wanted to shake her, sitting there so stubborn and resolute.

"No, thank you," she said sweetly, primly. "I really can't accept gifts from strangers." And she handed them back.

There was a muffled snort of laughter from Sean.

Paul felt heat creep along his neck and into his ears. He knew for a fact that he hadn't blushed in twenty years, not since Peggy Galaway kissed him in the hallway at school and his best friend had seen it. Yet, more than once since meeting Stassney, he had known a rush of blood to his face. It was unnerving.

"Take the damn things!" he gritted, practically flinging them at her.

She smiled, fluttering her lashes at him as she did. "Since you put it that way." And she placed the maligned sandals on the floor next to her sneaker-clad feet. "Are you ready to go?" she asked her driver, effectively dismissing the scowling man who stood next to the bright blue station wagon.

"Yes, ma'am." Sean put the car in gear and eased them through the village, dodging children, a few dogs and some noisy chickens. Paul stood in the middle of the track and watched them out of sight. His face wore a look of contained fury.

Stassney stared at the fields as Sean drove slowly by and explained what was going on in each one. Her mind wasn't on the crops; it was still back in the village, wondering what the agriculture expert was doing now. Probably out looking at those mysterious plants he was growing. Her eyes softened as she glanced at the sandals now in her possession."

"Coffee is grown in the shade of the taller trees," Sean was telling her. "It can't take the full sun."

"I see," she said.

"We also grow tea and cocoa and, of course, coconuts." He stopped torturing her with forced conversation after that and drove back to the house in silence.

Chapter Five

All the dinner guests had arrived. Stassney had met Claude and Renata Joliquin, a couple named Smith and several others, including an undersecretary in the Lands Department, Roger Natim. Other than herself, there were no single women. There were few unattached females, native or foreign, on the island, she realized.

"Looking at you is making my blood pressure go up," Sean said gallantly, leading her from one group of chatting couples to another. He apparently was her unofficial escort.

She smiled delightedly up at him. Her dress was raw silk, designed by Kim with a modestly plunging neckline in front and a daringly bold one in the back which dipped below her waist. The pale cream color almost matched her skin tones, and the total effect was saved from blandness by a brilliant or-

ange silk scarf that floated around her shoulders.
Her evening shoes were cream silk and her purse
was a brocade with orange flowers embroidered
into the material.

"Not wearing your new sandals, I see," he
teased, glancing down at her pumps showing beneath the long skirt of her dress.

Her smile didn't waver one bit as she shook her
head. She would rather not have been reminded of
Paul and his gift. "I prefer being as tall as possible.
You make me feel like a midget." Her eyes, art-
fully smudged with gray and silver liner, flirted up
at her tall companion. One thing she could be grate-
ful for—being a WAG had made her adept at social
repartee. She was completely poised in any society.

A movement on the terrace caught her eye. At
that moment, Paul walked into the large salon,
dressed in a white dinner jacket and looking so incredibly handsome that her breath disappeared. The
buttery sensation attacked her knees, and she clung
to Sean's arm as if to a lifeline.

"There's Paul," he said. "Let's go say hello. I
didn't think he would make it tonight." His eyes
swept to the woman who held on to his arm. He
chuckled softly. "I guess I should have known he
wouldn't be able to stay away."

Stassney was made uncomfortable by Sean's observation. Could everyone see at a glance the attraction between Paul and her? She had never had
as much trouble hiding her innermost feelings. Of
course, she had never had to hide them because she

hadn't had such severe emotional swings before in her life, other than the few difficult years after her father's death.

"Paul!" Raoul hurried forward to welcome his friend. The two men shook hands warmly, and Stassney sensed the underlying affection between them.

"Well, so glad you could make it," Leah said with just the right amount of warmth in her tones to cover the sardonic edge to the words. "I'll have the cook set an extra place."

Stassney had to grin as Leah's words effectively put Paul in his place. She thought only Paul, Raoul, Sean and she caught the verbal barb. It really was rude to show up for dinner without letting the hostess know for sure he was coming. A faint sweep of color highlighted his strong face, but his smile was wide and unabashed.

"Thank you, Leah," he murmured graciously, kissing her hand in a most courtly manner. "I couldn't resist your hospitality...."

"I know what you couldn't resist," Leah interrupted dryly. Without any subtlety whatsoever, she looked directly at Stassney.

Stassney felt her face going warm.

Paul laughed softly, his gaze also on her. "Now that you've succeeded in embarrassing both of us, how about some of that champagne punch your parties are famous for?"

Raoul led the way to the small bar where Stassney and Sean still stood. He poured a small glass

of the tart fruit punch which served as an appetizer
and handed it to Paul.

"Good evening," Paul said to the couple who
seemed to have taken root in the spot. Over the
edge of the punch cup, his gaze roamed over Stassney with debilitating thoroughness.

Her hair was up on top of her head with little
wisps drifting around her face and neck. He felt as
if he couldn't breathe as he gazed down on her
sheer perfection. Then his lungs really did stop
functioning as she turned to accept a refill on her
punch. There was no back to her dress!

He wanted to whip off his coat and cover her up
so no one else could see the provocative display of
satin skin against the silk of her outfit. He wanted
to carry her off into the jungle to some hidden glen
and remove every stitch of clothing she wore and
gaze his fill of her and then make love to her for
hours and hours without end. He could feel the
banked fires of desire fighting the restraint of his
will.

He shouldn't have come to this dinner party, he
thought, chastising his weakness. He had known
that even while he showered and shaved and made
himself presentable. Longing racked his lean, hard
frame. It was too late for recriminations. She was
inextricably ingrained in his memory.

In a few minutes, Leah, on the arm of the undersecretary, indicated it was time to go in to dinner. She seated Stassney next to Roger Natim. Paul
was on the opposite side of the table at the far end.

He knew it was Leah's way of punishing him for the past sins as well as present ones, and he grinned wryly at her revenge, which was very effective. He was so close to Stassney and yet so far away.

Again and again during the meal, he heard her laughter ring out as Roger told her amusing anecdotes from his experiences in the islands. Each time, his fingers closed tighter on his fork or the stem of delicate crystal when he glanced down the table and saw the attentive look on her face as she listened.

"Stassney?" Leah interrupted the conversation. "Did Roger tell you he went to Yale, too?"

Large brown eyes turned back to the native Papuan beside her. "Did you!" she demanded, a fresh smile blooming over her face.

Paul groaned internally. He might have known she went to some prestigious university like that. He heard Roger ask her when she had attended.

"I still am," she explained. "I'm working on my master's in chemistry. One last project and I'll be through."

"What are your plans after that?" Roger asked.

Stassney forced herself to concentrate on the man beside her. His smile gleamed in his coffee-colored face, and his hair was cut short, allowing it to curl naturally. He was cosmopolitan in his outlook on the world, realizing the enormous steps his country must make to become a self-sustaining part of the larger community of nations. She truly was fascinated by his plans for future development.

"I'd like to work in a research lab. Those jobs are rather hard to find, though, unless you're associated with a university or get a government grant. My mother wants me to teach. To please her, I got a double major in my undergraduate work—education and chemistry—and taught at the prep school for two years...."

"And you didn't like teaching?" Roger asked. He seemed very interested in her answer.

Renata Joliquin, seated next to Paul, tried politely to include him in the dinner conversation at that end of the table, but he didn't hear her question. He was completely attuned to the discussion going on between Stassney and Roger. With an understanding glance from the young man beside her down to the young woman across the table, Renata gave up and talked to her other neighbor.

"Teaching was okay. The kids were super. But it was the faculty and PTA meetings that got to me. And teaching isn't the same as doing research, although I don't mind it if I can also do the other."

"Have you taught any in college?"

Stassney nodded to her dinner partner, stray wisps of hair moving gently around her face. Her eyes seemed unusually large and gentle in the candlelight. "Yes, I have a teaching fellowship, in fact. The master's candidates get the lab classes and freshmen." Her soft laughter belied the complaining tone of voice as she explained her plight.

Paul moved restlessly in the comfortable chair. So she was going to school on a fellowship. It was still Yale. She probably knew hundreds of rich guys, dated them all the time, went to their big fancy houses on weekends. Look at how easy this dinner was for her. He frowned mightily, thinking of her backless dress. She was used to sophisticated clothes and parties...and a cushy existence.

Stassney tried to keep her eyes from going to Paul. It was hard. Every time she glanced down that way, he was scowling at her. Except for the times when he looked as if he wanted to devour her! Her neck felt hot as it had when she had been self-conscious as a child. She hoped no one noticed. That's rich, she mocked herself. As if everyone at the table hadn't noticed Paul's stare and the tension that arced between them like a visible cable.

Instead of a rest and recuperation period, this vacation was more likely to give her a nervous breakdown, she thought as anger built to higher levels inside her. If she got the chance, she was going to give Paul Windham a piece of her mind but good! Meeting his hard gaze, she directed a look of such quelling proportions at him that, for the space of thirty seconds, he looked away.

Finally, the meal was over.

Stassney, still held captive by Roger Natim, went with him back into the salon to have an after-dinner liqueur. He continued his questioning in greater depth.

"Would you consider returning here when you finish your studies?" he asked.

Stassney was totally unprepared for the question.

"Here?" she croaked. "You mean, on this island?"

"At the mainland. We're setting up an agriculture laboratory in Port Moresby and need people such as yourself to train our own people. There's also work in our growing oil, gold and silver industries." He smiled and moved his hands outward in an expansive gesture. "Take your pick of them."

Her heart was thumping with a loud drumbeat in her chest. A chance to stay here! To work in her field! She schooled herself to calmness. "I'm interested," she confessed. "I'd like to know more."

He invited her to come over to his office in Port Moresby so he could take her on a tour of their new facilities there and she could see for herself what they were doing.

"What's this?" Raoul demanded, breaking into the tête-à-tête that was earning curious glances from the other guests.

Roger explained the invitation.

"Perfect," he exclaimed. "I'm bringing Leah and Stassney over in a couple of weeks. We'll stop in." Raoul turned to Stassney. "You'd better say something to Paul before he explodes."

Startled, she swept the room with darkening eyes. Paul did resemble a thundercloud. He was standing next to Sean.

"What do you think?" Sean bent his flame-covered head toward the dark one of the shorter man as he waited for an answer.

"What?" Paul came out of his introspection

enough to realize that Sean had asked him something. "What? Oh, yes, the beans."

Sean sighed patiently. "Do you think we should...oh, never mind. I'll catch you tomorrow when your mind isn't so preoccupied with great and lofty matters."

Paul was watching Stassney come toward him. "Huh? Oh, yeah, sure. I'll see you tomorrow," he said, catching snatches of Sean's conversation.

Stassney stopped beside the two men. "Hello," she said softly. Her gaze was immediately locked into Paul's burning blue perusal.

At once he decided he would be as cool and sophisticated as she was. "You look beautiful tonight," he said, his eyes raking over her in a familiar fashion.

"Thank you," she said. Her expression was demure.

Paul tried to think of something else to say, something light and airy to explain why he had come to the dinner when he had told her that they wouldn't meet again. Desperately he nodded to Sean. "We were just talking about the winged beans."

Sean's laughter boomed out. "Leave me out of this," he said as he walked off.

An awkward, silent moment followed his departure. "Damn," Paul gritted. "Come on."

Taking Stassney's arm, he pulled her from the room. Out on the terrace, he released her as if he were being burned, and stepped back.

Stassney was so angry that she could hardly speak. "Just what is your problem?" she demanded. "You've stared at me all night."

He threw up his hands in disbelief. "You, of all people, can ask that?"

She turned on her heel and walked off the terrace and down the path to the low stone wall. He trailed after her, his long stride quiet on the flagstones, but she knew with every fiber of her body that he was there. The air was laden with floral scents, and suddenly it was hard for her to breathe again. She pressed a hand to her chest.

"Does it hurt for you to breathe?" he asked, full of concern for her.

"No," she snapped.

Paul stepped up beside her, raising one foot to rest on the wall. He was aware of her perfume, of the way the strands of hair wafted around her enchanting face, which was glowing in the moonlight, of her warm, womanly body so close to his.

His hand reached out, grasped the lower part of her face and turned it toward him. His lips met hers, which were parted and ready for him. He explored the treasure thoroughly.

His arms, going around her, encountered her bare back. His hands spread along the silky flesh, and memories of her beside him in the night came back to haunt him even as he held the reality of her close to him. "Stass, Stass," he whispered, wanting her with an aching heaviness in his loins.

Stassney couldn't help but respond to his tortured

murmur. Her arms went around his waist, and she clung to him even though she had vowed earlier to have nothing to do with this changeable male. Why should she put up with his scowls and accusing tone?

His hands roamed over her sides and hips, down along her thighs and back up over her buttocks, pausing to grasp the roundness there before returning to the enticing skin of her back, his to touch without cloth between. She felt herself being pulled into the whirlpool of his passion while her own sprang from deep inside her to meet every eddy of desire.

Turning her slightly, he eased a tiny space between them. While his mouth ravaged hers, his hand moved up her ribs until he cupped her breast. Slipping inside her gown, he took the fullness into his palm, savoring its heated heaviness as he felt it swell and bead from his touch. He was on fire, burning for her.

"Ummm," she made a little moaning sound, wanting him so much, wanting more from him, more than she had ever before wanted from a man. His caress was gentle yet demanding. He seemed to know exactly what to do to send her into ecstasy.

Abruptly, he thrust her from him and stepped back again. "Why couldn't you be like the rest of Leah's friends?" he growled, full of resentment for what she could do to him...and all of it against his will and better judgment. How had this madness happened to him? Why couldn't he control it?

Stunned, Stassney could only stand there, feeling helpless in the face of his unreasonable anger, then the burning rapture she had known in his arms turned into blazing fury as she realized the implications of his words.

"Let me remind you that Leah is my friend and most of her friends are also mine," she said with icy overtones. "Any insults you apply to them will be taken personally by me." There, she had made her position clear!

Strong hands grasped her shoulders. "You're not like them." He gave her a little emphatic shake. "If you were, you wouldn't be innocent. And I could take you without any qualms of conscience."

"I wish I knew some really good insulting names. I'd call you all of them."

He suggested a couple, his voice taunting her with her lack of knowledge along these lines.

Stassney ignored him. "You know something?... You really should be flattered by the fact that all the women fall for you. Instead of being so *above it all,* why don't you try a little compassion, see their side of it?"

"Those man-eaters!..."

"Kim isn't like that. Whatever she felt for you was genuine, and if you couldn't see that, why, then, you're...you're just blind!" She shook her head, impatient with him as he stonily glared down at her without responding to the accusation.

"And as for the other woman, the divorcée," she continued, "can't you understand that she had just gone through her second failure in marriage? That has to do something deep and drastic to a person's image of herself. Two failures! And in spite of the frequency of divorce, it's still considered a major shortcoming in our society.''

"And I was supposed to rebuild her shattered ego?'' he asked in scathing tones.

Stassney remembered her ex-steady. "No, not exactly, but you could have been more patient.'' But Leah had said he hadn't walked out on his birthday party after that embarrassing kiss. Maybe she was being too harsh. "Oh, I don't know what you should have done. Just don't glare at me all evening ever again!''

His unexpected chuckle was the final straw. She spun from him and started up the path. He caught her with gentle hands about her waist and pulled her back against him. "You're a magnet, and I'm only a piece of iron, drawn irresistibly toward you.''

"Hah!'' she scoffed. The buttons of his dinner jacket pressed intimately to the flesh along her spine as he held her in a close embrace. "You're just a poor, innocent farmer who keeps getting taken as a sex symbol by all those voracious women.'' Her voice dripped with mock pity.

He spoke in low, husky tones. "And how do you see me—as a farmer or a sex symbol?'' Slowly, he turned her until she faced him.

"Oh, I'm as bad as all the others. I see you as a man, strong, attractive...and definitely sexy.'' She was teasing, but there was an undertone of seriousness.

"You're the sexy one," he murmured, his mouth hovering close to hers. "The shape of your lips, the hidden passion in your eyes, the way your hair looks when it's all mussed." He drew a deep breath. "The sound of your laughter across the room, the little noises you make when I kiss you, the...."

"Stop it!" She pushed away from him, freeing herself from the torture of his arms, refusing to listen to his seductive praise of her. "Why are you doing this?" she asked.

He dropped his arms, clenching his fists at his sides. "Because for the first time in a long time, I want a woman. And I know I can't have you. That's the irony of it," he explained bitterly.

"Why can't you have me?" she asked in a whisper, fascinated by and afraid of his confession.

His fingers caressed her cheek and dropped back to his side. "Because you can't live my life and I can't live yours."

She was totally confused by his answer. She paced back to the low wall and sat on it, contemplating the man who glared out at the night with his hands jammed in his pockets and his shoulders set in stubborn lines. "You're impossible to understand," she complained.

"Not really." He propped one foot on the wall and leaned his forearm on his powerful thigh, his eyes taking in every curve of her pale figure that was outlined by the moonlight. The painful tightening in his body reminded him of how dangerous she was to his peace of mind. She had already invaded his defenses.

"Then explain yourself to me...in words of one syllable," she challenged. "I don't recall asking you to live with me, and I only needed shelter at your place for two nights, not a lifetime. And you were the one who decided I wasn't the type for an affair, remember?"

"Are you the type for an affair?" he asked softly.

"I don't know."

He sighed heavily. This was getting them nowhere. "Look, Stass, I was once engaged. Her name was Anne. She was twenty-one, a student at the university, when I met her. When I got the chance to come over here, I asked her to marry me and come, too. But she had one more year of school. She came over to visit me between quarters...once."

Stassney couldn't stop the start of surprise when he told her he had been engaged. It confirmed her worst fears—he had loved a woman and it hadn't worked out.

"At the end of her visit, I don't know who was in the greatest hurry—her to get to the airport or me to get her there. I watched a sweet, goodnatured woman turn into a nagging shrew right before my eyes," he continued. "She hated it here in the islands. I was stationed in Port Moresby then.

She didn't like the heat and humidity, the lack of shopping facilities, the apartment where I lived. It was a total disaster.''

Stassney saw the bright side to the situation. ''But at least you found out you weren't suited before you married. The two of you obviously didn't want the same things from life. You had different life-styles and requirements....''

''Exactly,'' he interrupted. ''Just as you and I do.''

She toyed with the ends of the silk scarf. ''How do you know?''

''I just do,'' he said irrefutably. ''What did you think of the hut?''

She considered the question carefully. ''It was romantic for two nights. Longer than that and I would probably think of it as merely primitive,'' she said honestly.

''Yes,'' he said. He turned and sat beside her, his long legs stretched out beside her shorter ones. He seemed to be studying them as if the length of their limbs exposed the basic differences between the people.

''But an adult doesn't expect constant romance, Paul. I know life isn't like that. Living together, establishing a home, working at interesting, productive careers—these things are important to me, not the circumstances surrounding them. I don't mind simple living arrangements.''

''You say that now, but it's easy when you've always lived a life of luxury.''

"A life of luxury! I'll have you know I have always worked for what I got. During my undergraduate years, I worked for a swimming pool company, testing home pools and adding chlorine or acid as needed, in the summers. During the winter, I worked in the school lab as a lab assistant, which is mostly a glorified title for a flunky. I went to school on a scholarship...the same as you did, Leah said."

"Yes, but look where you went, the people you associated with all of your life. You're *used* to wealth."

"And you're making a class distinction between us where none exists," she said angrily. Who would have ever thought she would be sitting on a wall, surrounded by jungle, thousands of miles from her home, and arguing about her background with a man who attracted her more than any she had ever met? She was afraid to use the word love for her feelings for Paul. That would open her to hurt that she wasn't yet ready to face. "This is ridiculous."

He stood. "You're right. There's no use in talking about something that I knew was impossible right from the start. Tell Leah I enjoyed the dinner and I appreciate her setting an extra place for me." He stepped over the wall and started down a dark path toward the fields below.

To Stassney, he looked unsubstantial, ghostly, as he moved swiftly away from her. Even so, she could still feel the pull of tension between them. The emotional level that had developed in just a

few short days was deep. She felt she knew him
better than she had ever known anyone else in her
life. Kindred souls, she thought, a slight smile lifting the lines of her lips. Paul felt it, too. And resented the fact.

"I'll still be your friend, if you don't want to be
lovers," she called after him on an impulse. Let
him think about that! she seethed to herself, going
back to the house.

Paul threw back the sheet and got out of bed. It
was after midnight, he noted as he pulled on a pair
of jeans and a shirt. *She* had probably been asleep
for hours, he thought with an angry tug at his socks
as he jerked his running shoes on. He walked out
to the covered front porch on the two-bedroom
guesthouse and gazed up at the big house. A light
was on, shining dimly through the darkness like a
beacon just for him.

He was aware of the void in his life. When Anne
had left, he had gone back to his empty apartment
and sleepless nights and vowed never to get caught
in the tender trap of a woman's arms again. Now,
only two nights with Stassney and he was prowling
about with a restless loneliness that was unlike anything he had ever experienced before.

He banged the heel of his fist softly against the
railing around the porch. He would be a fool to get
mixed up with her. When she went back to her
world—as she would—he would be left standing at

the pier, longing for a dream that would never return, lost in his own private cult of hell.

What was it about her? She wasn't the prettiest woman he had ever seen...although she was beautiful with her large eyes that hid a smoldering passion in their depths as well as a fountain of tenderness. She was smart, obviously, and she had an inner core of femininity that couldn't be obscured by her drive to succeed in her field.

He could use a chemist, he realized. All those soil tests and experiments he did for nutrient requirements of the plants he was working with. Would she like to do that?

God, what was he thinking? If Anne, who had been born to the ranching life, couldn't take his way of living, how could Stassney? That day she arrived, when she lost her purse, she said she hated the islands. Of course, she had been exhausted and worried at that moment. He smiled involuntarily, remembering her buoyant spirit and her refusal to be frightened for long by either him or the jungle. She has a good mind, he thought, capable of making sound judgments. And a will to face and overcome difficulties. She had truly been wonderful on that long, dark climb. Uncomplaining, not saying a word when she had cut her foot.

His eyes narrowed on the lighted window. Was that her room? It was in the guest wing of the house. Without making a conscious decision, he stepped off the porch and started up the path. He took a shortcut through the coconut palms, ignoring the fact that he could be risking a concussion if one of the ripening nuts fell on his head. It was an event that had happened before in the area.

He walked rapidly through the grove and then up the incline to the terraced level. He stopped outside her door.

Yes, she was there, sitting on a lounge chair, looking beautiful in a flowing gown and robe of some gossamer material, while she read a book. His mouth felt dry as he lifted his hand and knocked softly on the door. He watched as her head jerked up at the sound. Then she was rising, laying the book aside, and coming to the door.

Stassney stared at Paul as if he were an intruder. "What are you doing here?"

He rocked back on his heels, and, tilting his head slightly to one side, drawled, "Where else could I be with you up here? It was lust at first sight."

She didn't fail to see the seriousness in his eyes in spite of his bold teasing. She responded to the latter. "Speak for yourself." Her grin was impudent.

The smile on his lips matched hers. "I am. I want you." He lifted a hand to her hair, brushing it away from her temple as if he were searching for the very best spot to kiss her. His eyes delved into hers. "I want you for a lover."

"Not a friend?" she questioned, keeping the smile on her face.

He shrugged. "That, too."

Stassney slowly pivoted from the door and retreated into her room. Paul followed, closing the door with a decisive click behind them. His gaze stayed on her, its blue intensity flustering her already ragged nerves. She wanted so much more than mere lust from him, she realized. Because she felt so much more for him.

Sometimes love was like that, sneaking up on a person, without warning. One minute you thought you were in total control, the next you knew you were hopelessly lost.

When had it happened? At the first glance? During the hard climb to the hut when he had given so much of himself to her in terms of strength and gentleness and understanding? When he had shared his bed, his food and his malaria tablets with her?

"Well?" he demanded.

As if she could make a life-changing decision at the snap of the fingers! She let her gaze take in the exquisite room with its rich furnishings and comfortable amenities. She pictured the grass hut on its stilts with its stark necessities. Neither place seemed real to her.

"I...I don't know," she said softly.

"How old are you?"

"Twenty-five."

His eyes trapped her gaze, refusing to let her escape from the knowledge of their mutual desire. "You're old enough."

"For an affair?" Her voice quavered, and she heard the contradiction between the words and the tone.

His face hardened. "Yes. You were the one who indicated you could handle it." His imagination pictured her at the guesthouse, lying on his bed, softly mussed from their lovemaking. And then he thought of how it would be when she was gone...the empty bed, the silence that echoed with her laughter and passionate murmurs.

Stassney saw pain flash through Paul's eyes. Was he thinking of Anne? "Why did it seem impossible to you earlier but feasible now?" she asked as if they were discussing a business deal instead of the intimate sharing of themselves.

Bending, he lifted her into his arms and sat in a delicate chair, enfolding her in a cradled embrace. His nose nuzzled along her ear, sniffing the shampoo and perfume in her hair. "I slept two nights with a beautiful woman and I've spent two sleepless nights without her. Which situation would you choose, given a choice?" he asked in his lazy drawl that was incredibly sexy.

"Alone,' she promptly replied, striving for the light touch. "I can't sleep with other people."

"You slept with me." His lips did tantalizing things to the skin along her neck.

"Because I was tired."

"You'll be tired," he promised, amused with her evasions. "Come home with me."

The husky invitation hung on the air, echoing over and over in her mind. She was so tempted. To lie beside him, to know his complete touch, to learn the things that pleased him stirred a deep well of longing within her.

"I can't. I'm a guest here. Of Leah." She grasped for straws to help her past this hurdle. It was so hard to think when he was touching her...like that, as his hand explored her side, stopping to press a palm alongside her breast before sliding over to cup the gently mounded weight entirely.

"Leah will understand." He licked a spot along her collarbone, and she gasped in surprise at the sensation it caused. "We're natural together, do you see that?" His voice held a trace of amazement in it, as if it had never been this way before for him.

"Will our children?"

He raised his head, his face solemn with promise. "I'll take care of you."

She closed her eyes as her will to resist this alluring male slipped a little more. He wanted her. They could have this time together, she thought feverishly. She loved him. Would his desire balance her love, or would one overpower the other, leaving hate and hurt in its wake?

She didn't know the answer, and it wasn't something she could test out in the lab. Life had to be lived; love had to be shared.

A soft knock sounded on the hall door. Blue eyes and brown ones flashed as one in that direction.

"Stassney?" Leah called in low tones. "Are you all right?"

A small panic touched Stassney's face as she looked up at Paul. He nodded his head at her.

"Yes, I...I'm fine. I was reading. Am I bothering you?"

"No, I just saw the light on and wondered if you were ill." Leah's voice showed her concern.

"No, I'm fine. Really."

"Okay. Good night. Sleep as late as you want in the morning."

"Yes, I will. Thank you."

Stassney sighed in relief when her friend went on.

"What was she doing up at this hour?" Paul muttered. "Never mind." He dipped his head, intending a thorough exploration of the lips that enticed him without mercy. "Stass, kiss me," he ordered, his arms tightening, pulling her close, wanting her.

"Let me go, Paul," she requested.

"You don't mean that." He held her closer.

"Yes, I do. I need...time to think." It was impossible to think logically with his mouth touching the corner of her lips in erotic forays that made her feel as if she were drowning.

"Don't think," he whispered.

She let herself enjoy the kiss. For just a few seconds, she allowed the fantasy to bloom that this was right, that being in his arms was part of forever, that he loved her as she loved him. But neither a fantasy nor the reality of being held and kissed passionately could block out the truth from her innate honesty.

Holding a steady pressure against his shoulders, she refused to melt into him or deepen the embrace. As she had that night in his bed when he gave her the good-night kiss, she simply held it at the level it had begun.

Finally he raised his head. "No?" he questioned, his eyes dark with his desire for her, bringing an answering flame in hers. With one finger, he drew the outline of her lips, loving the finely carved shape, the succulent feast he found in her mouth. "I love kissing you," he murmured, making her senses go dizzy once again.

"Don't," she whispered, her throat aching with the effort.

"You want me."

"Yes, but..."

He sighed deeply, causing his chest to lift against hers, bringing her breasts into pressure-sensitive contact with his warmth. "How much time?" At her bemused look, he demanded. "How much time do you need to think? A day, a week, the rest of the month? How long will you be here, anyway?"

"Another month after this one," she answered the last question, but her thoughts were all on the first.

"Seven weeks," he said, thinking aloud.

If he took her with him on his trips when he stayed at the huts, would she last even seven days? he wondered. If she stayed the entire time with him, would he be able to give her up when she really had to go back? After she got her degree, would she be willing to come back here and work with him? A knife blade of agony stabbed through him. What if she ended up hating him as Anne had done?

"What is it?" Stassney asked, worried about the expression in his eyes as he stared down at her, his arms tight around her as if he would bind her to him until their flesh blended.

"Life is a question mark," he said on a cynical note. He sighed again and stood up, letting her legs slip to the floor until she was standing, too. Then he moved away from her, prowling the room like a jungle creature prowling the night.

He had one more year on his current contract; then he would be free to go back to the States. Would Stassney still be free then? Or would she have met someone else? Time. He needed time to strengthen her physical attraction for him into something more lasting. Would she really be able to accept the life-style he could provide even if they lived in the States and he went to work for some big agribusiness company?

Stassney watched the play of emotion in Paul's face and hurt for him. "Tell me what's bothering you," she pleaded, going to him and laying a hand on his arm.

He looked at her hand, the slender fingers with their well-kept nails and the college ring. His glance roamed the rest of her, taking in the silk nightgown and robe, the room that fitted her so well with its rich furnishings, and knew it was hopeless.

Turning from her, he went to the door. In the small squares of glass, he could see her reflection, surrounded by the room's luxury. This was where she belonged. To think anything else was the product of a deluded mind, he reminded himself harshly.

His hand reached for the doorknob. "Good-bye, Stass." And they both heard the finality in the word. He opened the crystal-paned door and left.

Chapter Six

Stassney learned a lot about island life during the next two weeks. The spring and fall seasons were the crop-growing periods in the tropics, and the villagers raised kau-kau, a yam that was their principal food, some green vegetables and breadfruit. Their houses were made from kona-grass, which was really a type of palm. They liked to wear necklaces made from dogs' teeth, and they used magic stones, which looked like doughnuts, as lethal weapons.

Raoul kept up with his international interests through a radio-phone link to the outside world. He and Sean were very busy with the fall planting season.

"These are the winged beans that Paul mentioned," Sean explained to Stassney while they were on an extended tour of the plantation.

Leah spoke up from the back of the station

wagon where she and Raoul sat. "They're the most versatile vegetable you can imagine."

Sean nodded. "You can eat them like green beans or even in a salad when they are small. We harvest them when the beans are mature. They are to the tropics what the soybean is to the temperature zones of the world. And they're as nutritious."

"Maybe more. They generally have more protein," Raoul said.

"I've never heard of them. Were they recently discovered?" Stassney was interested in this wonder food.

"No," Sean told her. "They've been known for a long time, but they're considered the poor man's staple because they grow wild and are used mostly when other food sources aren't available. We're trying to overcome that prejudice."

"I see," she murmured.

Leah tapped her on the shoulder. "Paul has convinced some of the local women to try adding the pods to lizard stew. Now it's become a prestige thing to come up with new dishes to try out on your neighbors when you invite them to a singsing."

"Singsing?" Stassney questioned.

Sean and Raoul spoke together. "A corroboree."

"A social gathering," Leah said, explaining both words, the Papuan and the Australian, for a dinner and entertainment evening. "There's feasting…"

"Lizard stew with winged beans," Sean tossed in.

"…music and dancing…"

"Seduction in the moonlight," Raoul added.

"Will you two shut up!" Leah demanded while the other three laughed. "You'll give Stassney the wrong impression."

"I'm impressed," Stassney declared. "It sounds like a wonderful orgy. I can hardly wait to attend. Will we be invited to one, do you think?"

"Probably," Leah said dryly. "Every time Paul suggests something new, the villagers throw a party for him."

Stassney pictured Paul as he had been in the village that day, wearing cutoffs and sandals; then she saw him at Leah's dinner, dressed in white jacket and dark slacks. He moved easily from one world to the other, she thought.

She tried not to think of him, but he invaded her dreams every night. She wondered if his sleep was as restless as hers now was. How could two nights change her life so drastically? A sad smile touched her lips briefly. Her swearing off of men had lasted only until her first sight of him. After four years of holding men at a friendly distance, she was now haunted by a chance encounter with one devastating male.

Physically, she was much better. She rarely coughed now, and she could go for long walks with Leah without becoming breathless on the slightest incline. Her skin tone had deepened from cream to light tan from afternoons sunbathing on the terrace.

She had attended a round of teas and card parties and dinners in her honor at the other plantations on the island. The activities were pleasant and undemanding...and she was already becoming bored. She needed more of a challenge in her life, some task that taxed her wits and ingenuity or at least gave her a sense of accomplishment.

"Roger has planned a dance at the club for you when we go over to Port Moresby. We got a message from him today, and we'll go over tomorrow," Leah said when they arrived back at the house. She followed Stassney to her bedroom. "I'm going to the doctor there," she confided.

Stassney whirled, worry furrowing her brow. Her expression lightened, and then a wide grin spread over her face at the smug look on her friend's face. "You're pregnant," she concluded.

Leah nodded, almost shy now that the secret was out. "Don't say anything yet. I want to be sure."

"I won't," Stassney promised. "Does Raoul suspect?"

"Yes," Leah said softly. "He notices any changes in me right away."

They laughed together, two friends who had been close for many years.

The next day they left for Port Moresby, catching an island freighter, then a seaplane, and arriving at the capital city as evening fell. Roger Natim sent a car to take them to their hotel, which Stassney thought was very nice.

"He's wooing you," Raoul said, his meaning not lost on the two women. "He wants you working in one of the labs. You'll probably head up a group."

"I'd certainly consider it," Stassney said. She avidly watched the street scenes as the car slowly made its way along narrow streets.

It was Sunday, and the port and town proper seemed subdued compared to the first evening she had spent there. It was the day for worship, not play or work, she realized, seeing people making their way into the buildings.

She noted when two people walked together, they often shared the carrying of a parcel, even if it was a purse.

"It's the island way," Leah explained.

Stassney felt the smart of tears in her eyes. She was touched by this simple act of human sharing, she realized. The islanders' willingness to help with another's burdens indicated the good that existed in community life.

"Here we are," Leah said.

They got out and entered a hotel that was beautiful and as modern as any in New York.

After a quiet dinner, the three travelers went to their rooms. Roger was to pick Stassney up in the morning, and she was to spend the day in his company while Raoul and Leah took care of their business. Then they were to meet at a resort club for dinner and entertainment later.

"After you've had a good, long nap," Leah decided, sounding very maternal.

Stassney went to bed, full of anticipation for the coming day.

She wasn't disappointed when the sun rose. The

temperature was a pleasant seventy-five degrees, and the air held a springtime crispness, as if the seasons had gotten reversed. She washed and dressed and rushed downstairs to the sound of the *lali,* the split-gong that heralded the new day.

The natives said the day started here in the Pacific, and they were right. The international date line ran through the area. Back in Connecticut, it was still Sunday. Her mother was living in the past, she thought with a smile as she went into the dining room.

Raoul and Leah weren't up yet, but she wasn't the only early diner. Paul sat at a table by the open window, reading a paper, the remains of his breakfast pushed to one side.

Stassney paused, not sure whether to speak or not. She had only caught fleeting glimpses of him since that night he had come to her room. She decided to ignore him as he had been doing to her. And still was. Just as she swerved toward a booth in the far corner from him, he looked up.

The entire blue of the sky seemed concentrated in his eyes as he quickly skimmed over her neat sundress with its short-sleeved jacket of mint green. The dress was white, and both it and the jacket were edged with identical floral bands at the neck and hem. Her shoes were a practical wedge-heeled mesh, made for walking, and her purse was a straw bag of island design. He thought she looked like a New England flower transplanted to a tropical setting.

"Join me?" he invited in a husky tone. He had to swallow hard before he could follow the words with a smile. She was so beautiful that he could barely stand to look at her.

For a second, she considered refusing, but then she found herself nodding and accepting a chair that he pulled out for her. She sat opposite him and perused the menu, trying not to glance across the table at his masculine perfection. He wore jeans and a chambray shirt. She wondered what he was doing here. And how he got in. He hadn't been on the island shuttle.

"How did you get to town?"

"Seaplane," he explained briefly. "I've been here a couple of days, getting information for a new project." He sipped coffee while the waiter took Stassney's order. "What are you doing?"

"I came over for some sightseeing with Raoul and Leah. Roger Natim is going to give me a tour while they do some business." She wasn't going to tell him that she was considering working here. Replacing the morning menu in its slot, she glanced around the room. Flowers and potted plants were strategically located in order to lend an air of tropical abundance to the place. Hibiscus bloomed in an informal hedge outside the window, and an ornate bird feeder swung gently to and fro on the early morning breeze.

Paul cleared his throat as if he had an announcement to make. She looked at him.

"I want to apologize for the other night in your room," he said.

"Why?" Her brow lifted in surprise.

"I came on like a...well, too strong, at any rate. I had no right barging in and making that kind of demand of you, and...I'm sorry," he finished softly.

She shrugged one shoulder, indicating it didn't matter. "I *have* been doing a lot of thinking," she began then stopped.

"And?"

Her smile was brief. "I still don't know."

His strong hand waved the problem aside. "Forget it."

"You've changed your mind?" she asked.

His eyes narrowed, looked over her with a smoldering caress. "I want you so much right this minute that I ache with it. Does that answer your question?"

"Yes." Her voice was shaky.

He leaned back in his chair with a smile. "You're looking very lovely this morning, Miss Stassney Murdock."

She loved the teasing note he settled on as he looked her over once more. He had such a wealth of character and personality. There were depths in him, but his control was a sure thing, not letting his emotions or libido get out of control. A man that a woman could trust in every situation. He wouldn't take advantage. Remembering the night in her room, she almost wished he had. It was much easier to be seduced than have to take the responsibility of making a decision.

"Why haven't I seen you during the past two weeks?" she asked, feeling comfortable doing so. She knew she wouldn't get a put-down from him.

"I'm not going to make it easier for you. I'm not going to seduce you," he stated flatly, drawing a startled jerk from her.

"Do you read minds?" she demanded.

"Only yours. You're as transparent as glass." He chuckled at her pronounced dismayed reaction. "Your eyes are readable...."

"I won't look at you ever again."

"And you have a lot of body language," he whispered seductively.

"You sounded very final when you left my room," she reminded him.

"And I meant it then." He grinned, looking suddenly young and endearing to her. "But I have only to see you and I'm under your spell again, brown eyes."

"My ego just grew three sizes," she told him, grinning back for all she was worth.

Her breakfast came then, interrupting the intimate conversation. Just in time, she thought, buttering a piece of whole wheat toast and adding jelly before taking a big bite. Where were they now? Back to square one, apparently. Back to that friendly level of companionship they had shared at the grass hut. Could they stay there? Well, she would give it a try.

"Paul, I'd like for us to be friends. Just friends."
She waited for his reaction.

"I'd like that, too, Stass."

Their eyes met and held, hers questioning, his assuring. It gave her the strangest feeling, as if they were committing to more than they were saying. But what?

"Don't worry about it," he said, knowing her better than she knew herself, it seemed.

After she had eaten, then had a second cup of coffee, she had to go to her room to finish preparations for her tour. She hated saying good-bye to Paul, but she did. He said he had to go to a meeting that morning with the government representatives on a new project he wanted to start on Lyra if the villagers were willing. She was interested immediately but asked no questions. She saw him cross the lobby and go out the door as she stepped into the elevator.

The car arrived promptly for her at ten. She had seen Leah and Raoul, talking to them while they had their breakfast and promising to return early that afternoon for her rest period. Then, the friendly driver had chatted with her as he drove her to the offices of the Department of Lands and Environment. Roger Natim was waiting at the door for her. Taking her elbow, he guided her into his own office, introducing her to his secretary who was from Tonga and was also his fiancée.

"Tonga, not Tanga," Leni said, smiling as the confusion cleared from Stassney's face. "It's an island group farther to the east of here. We're mostly Polynesians there.''

She was tall and slender with softly curling hair that framed a face of delicate contours. Stassney watched as Leni brought hot tea and biscuits into Roger's office then went out and closed the door behind her.

''She's lovely. She should be painted,'' Stassney said.

Roger beamed. He poured the tea then invited her to look at his butterfly specimens while it cooled. ''Only South America can rival us for color and variety, but nobody can rival us in size. Our Queen Alexandra birdwing butterfly is the largest in the world. ''It's listed in the Guinness Book.''

Stassney looked at the one he pointed out in a glass-covered case. It really was as large as a bird. Its two upper wings spanned eleven inches and were mostly black with soft yellow markings. The lower wings were light yellow with black dots and edges. There was a patch of brilliant red on the throat, while the body repeated the creamy yellow tones.

''We also have the largest moth, the largest stick insect and''—his grin now became a grimace— ''…the largest grasshopper. Our Insect Farming and Trading Project was started back in 1974 in only three provinces. Now we have butterfly ranches in more than ten provinces,'' he finished proudly.

Stassney loved the idea of a butterfly ranch. It

sounded like total folly, but a romantic one, she mused. "I'd like to visit one of these ranches."

"We will arrange it for your next visit," he promised. "Now it is time to tour the new lab facilities. You realize that not everything is built or installed yet?"

She nodded, understanding that he didn't want her to expect too much and be disappointed. They spent the rest of the morning out at a construction site. At noon, Roger was approached by a thin, wiry man with a worried air about him. They conversed for several minutes, then Roger turned a regretful face to Stassney.

"I am sorry, but something has come up that requires my immediate attention. A meeting on one of our new projects," he explained as they drove back to the office. "There is opposition that I must take steps to stem...." His voice trailed off in obvious concern.

Political problems were the same the world over, Stassney realized. Win some, lose some.

At the steps of the building, they met Paul.

Roger seemed relieved. "Did you talk to the committee?"

"Yes," Paul replied. "You're needed, though." He glanced at Stassney. "I'm going to see Rairi. I can take her off your hands for the rest of the afternoon."

"Ah, perfect." Roger was delighted. "This is your chance to see the butterfly ranch," he explained.

Smiling, she accepted the switch in escorts, not sure that she was all that pleased.

"What's wrong?" Paul asked, guiding her into the car and directing the driver to take them to the airport.

"I feel like the buck that's been passed," she said.

He chuckled, settling into the back seat beside her as the car shot forward. "You'll like this," he promised.

They took a short flight to another airport and then a Jeep into the hilly country enclosing a rain forest. The road was dusty, and the vehicle bounced agilely over the ruts.

"Is it very far?" she quipped. "I sure hope we don't have to walk."

Their eyes met in a brief look of shared experience, then Paul turned his attention back to the road as he turned onto a one-lane track that led into the forest. He stopped at a complex of six houses. The villagers came out to welcome them.

"Rairi is a butterfly rancher," Paul said, introducing her to the village leader. "We're going to discuss some of the aspects of growing the insects, and I'm going to introduce the idea to the people on Lyra."

A small stool was brought for her, while the rest of the people sat on woven mats. There was a respectful quiet as Paul and Rairi talked. When the discussion ended, there was a general dispersal.

Rairi brought out a box of paper envelopes and showed the contents to Stassney.

She exclaimed as each one was opened to reveal an individual butterfly. The colors were vivid—green, black, red, orange, yellow, white, blue—all were beautiful with iridescent tones and striking markings.

"These are top quality," Paul explained to her. "They're to be sent to collectors all over the world. And to students at colleges for their specimen studies. Scientific data will be sent with each one, identifying its type, habits and location where found."

"Mak'm two hundred dolla," Rairi said proudly, pointing to his cache. He told her the scientific names of several of the butterflies and got a book to show her their pictures in it. He knew what he was talking about.

In a few minutes, one of the women approached them, and the chief invited them to eat. Stassney was glad, for she had had no lunch. Again she was awarded the honor of the stool. Paul grinned up at her from his place on the mat. She smiled back, very happy.

The meal was simple but filling. There was kaukau, baked in coals and served on a small mat with a round bread roll. A bowl contained a sort of stew. She refused to think of lizard while she ate it.

On the trip back to the airport, she couldn't resist asking, "What was the stew made from? It wasn't lizard, was it? Sean said the women made lizard stew."

"No, it wasn't lizard."

"Good." They rode along in comfortable-but-jostled silence for a few minutes. Then, "What do you think it was?" she asked.

"Echidna," Paul said.

"Oh. What's that?"

"Spiny anteater."

She beat on his shoulder as he started laughing. "You beast! That was a terrible thing to say. Well, it was good stew, whatever it was made from," she declared with a satisfied smile as she settled back to enjoy the ride.

The short flight back to the port city took very little time, and Paul took Stassney back to the hotel right away. "Take a nap," he advised. "I'll see you at dinner...."

"We're going to some resort," she interrupted.

He grinned. "Didn't I tell you? I'm your date for the evening." She went to her room and lay down, afraid to go to sleep, afraid that when she woke up, she would find that she was dreaming.

Chapter Seven

The resort club had a raised stage for the floor-show and a small area in front of it for dancing. The linen-covered tables formed a series of semicircles that filled the rest of the dimly lit room. On one wall, a four-masted sailing schooner seemed to be sailing into port, the mural done so that the water appeared to be actually moving around the hull of the ship.

In spite of the tropical touches, all resorts felt the same to Stassney, as if they had been done by the same decorator who had been determined to create an atmosphere of intimate gaiety. She liked kona-grass huts better, she thought and was promptly ashamed of herself.

Their large table occupied one section by itself and was laden with bowls and baskets of fruits and flowers. They were served drinks with flaming sugar cubes on them and a delicious assortment of seafood and local vegetables for the meal. Roger had obviously made special arrangements for them, and he and Leni were a lovely host and hostess to the other two couples.

"We averted the crisis," Roger confided to Stassney over coffee.

Her interested glance invited him to explain in more detail if he wished. She assumed he meant the meeting earlier that day.

"Several factions would like to go to a commercial production of butterflies, a factory-type operation like that used in Taiwan and Korea. You get novelty store products that way—common specimens with paper-thin bodies, not fit for study." He shook his head in disgust with the idea.

Paul spoke up. "Roger and the DLE are trying to maintain the quality that the Papuan butterflies and moths have become known for."

"Did you talk the committee out of issuing a permit for the factory?" Raoul asked.

"Yes, thanks to Paul, we made it one more time," Roger said with a weary grin. He turned to Leni. "Enough of government problems. Would you care to dance?"

Leah and Raoul joined the other couple on the dance floor, leaving Paul and Stassney at the table. She pretended to be interested in her drink. A strong hand removed the frosty glass from her grasp. Paul took her hand in his and gently tugged her from her chair. She was strangely reluctant to be in his arms.

"Scared?" he asked near her ear after enfolding her within his embrace.

"Ummhmm," she admitted.

"Why?"

"Because when you hold me, I want to be more than just friends, but I don't think that's wise."

He placed her hand on his shoulder so he could put both arms around her while they danced, thus molding their bodies even closer. "Yes," he murmured. "I tell myself to stay away from you, but when I see you, all I want to do is kiss you and hold you...and make love to you." His lips deposited tiny kisses along her temple.

Although his hands stayed circumspectly at her waist, she felt the arousal of his body as their thighs brushed intimately in the closeness of the dance. Her heartbeat increased in tempo.

"There's a spot on your neck where, if I touch it with my lips, I can feel your pulse," he whispered huskily. "God, Stass, but I want you."

She wanted him, too, but she was compelled to tell him the truth. "Paul?" Raising her head, she looked into his eyes, willing him to understand what she was going to say. "Remember you said that you didn't want attachments and I said I didn't come with strings? I've done a lot of thinking about that, and...well, I think that's not true."

"Do you come with strings?" he asked on a deep note. His eyes roamed over her up-turned face, almost making her forget what she was trying to say.

She nodded slowly. "I think that if we made

love, then, in my heart, I would be committed to you. I'd feel married.''

He was silent for a long time, moving them around the crowded floor with practiced ease. Finally he spoke, "Yes, you're the type."

That's all he said for the rest of the dance. Stassney wasn't sure how to take the remark. She glanced at him as they went back to the table, but he was deep in his own thoughts, and she hadn't a clue as to what they were. This maddening uncertainty about his feelings was very hard to live with, she found.

But what was there to be uncertain about? He wanted her...without attachments. What could be simpler?

"Stassney, look! There's Carter," Leah exclaimed, grabbing Stassney's arm. "He hasn't been here in over a year."

The six at the table watched as a handsome man in his late forties entered the dining room and glanced around. He saw Leah and Stassney and smiled broadly, coming quickly toward them.

"Carter, what are you doing in this part of the world?" Leah demanded after receiving a kiss from him.

"Looking for you two," he replied, turning to Stassney and kissing her cheek. "Your mother told me to spank you, but you look too delectable for anything so brutal. She said she had only gotten one postcard and one brief letter since you left home three weeks ago."

"I meant to drop her a line today but didn't get around to it," she mumbled rather like an embarrassed school girl. She felt foolish as she met the surprisingly cold look Paul was giving her. His smile was cynical as Leah introduced Carter Remington to the group.

"Well, are you enjoying yourself?" Carter demanded as soon as a chair had been brought over for him.

"Yes," Stassney said, grinning at him with a surge of affection. He was her godfather and she had loved him all her life, turning to him with her problems after her father had died. He had been in love with her mother for years. "When did you see Mother? How was she? Did she get over her cold?"

"I saw her last week and she was fine, except for being irritated with one wayward daughter." His smile took away the barb in his words. "She asked me to check on you when I flew down to join the crew, so I called Ridgecrest and was told you were here at Port Moresby. Your hotel clerk said he saw you leave earlier and suggested this place as a possibility."

"Have you had dinner?" Leni asked politely. "The seafood platter is excellent."

"Yes, thank you," he replied cordially.

Stassney thought Carter had never looked better. With his solid silver hair and impeccable manners, dressed in a tailored dinner suit, he was urbane and cultured. A good catch. She wondered why her mother hadn't fallen in love with him. She thought

she would have. Her eyes went to Paul, and her
smile faded a bit. Why did people always fall in
love with someone who didn't want them? Her
mother and Paul would make a team, both of them
afraid of deeper relationships.

Paul afraid? Her mother scared to trust a man
again, to be dependent? She nibbled at the inside
of her lip, wondering if this could be true. No, they
were too strong, too sure of themselves. They didn't
need anybody.

Someone finished a funny story, and she laughed
with the rest, her gaze returning to her godfather.
She experienced an anguished wave of sympathy
for him and his unrequited love. Being in love, she
thought, made you more sensitive to other people's
happiness. She smiled sadly to herself. So it wasn't
all bad, after all.

When they rose to leave, she caught Paul studying her with a brooding quality in his expression.

Carter invited them to his ship for a nightcap,
and there was a general murmur of assent. They
followed him to the private pier in front of the resort.

"Have you been wheeling and dealing in this
part of the world?" Stassney asked him, tucking
her arm into his and automatically assuming the
role of hostess as they boarded the sparkling white
ship that required a crew of fifty to keep it ship-
shape. "Or is this one of your escapes from the
humdum of the office?"

"Business. I'm investing in a gold mine," he explained.

"I'd better talk to you about get-rich-quick schemes," she teased.

At the top of the gangplank, she led the guests to the salon, while Carter called his steward. In a few minutes, they were seated on expensively upholstered sofas, a crystal chandelier swaying with the gentle roll of the sea above their heads, and chatting amiably.

The steward placed the serving tray in front of Stassney, who called him by name as she greeted him with open friendliness. She poured tea for the women while the men opted for brandy. After one glance at Paul, she carefully concentrated her attention on the other members of the party.

Although his mouth was smiling, his mood was furious. She wondered if anyone else could tell. Her eyes met Leah's. Her friend raised her brows, glanced pointedly at Paul and shrugged. So she, too, could see something was wrong with him. With a silent sigh, Stassney joined in the conversation, her long training in deportment coming to her aid.

"I'd like a visit with you girls, uh, women," Carter corrected at a frown from Leah. Grinning, he continued, "Why don't you let me take you back to Lyra on the ship? It would be a pleasant two-day trip."

"That sounds wonderful. Raoul?" Leah questioned her husband on his business obligations.

"Fine with me," he agreed.

"Paul, will you join us?" Carter invited.

"I don't think…"

"Why don't you?" Roger interrupted the refusal. "We're through here, and you could use a break."

"That's almost an order," Leni said in a jovial warning.

The dark brows drew together in a slight frown over the blue eyes. "I don't want to impose," he said. He realized how stiff and awkward his statement sounded. Like an inexperienced kid, he groaned to himself.

"No trouble," Carter assured him. "There are plenty of beds."

Stassney couldn't stop her eyes from going to Paul. His flicked to her at the same time. Oh, lord, mention the word "bed" and they automatically look at each other, she thought, stifling a hysterical giggle.

There was a brief silence. "That's settled then," Carter announced. "We'll get underway at ten in the morning, so be here on time." His mock stern glance went to the two women whose habits he was quite familiar with.

"We will," they promised in chorus.

Stassney didn't see Paul at breakfast. She had a feeling that he wouldn't show up for the cruise, either. There would be a message that he had gotten tied up on some aspect of his many agricultural concerns and couldn't make the trip. It was with an uncustomary heaviness of spirit that she climbed in the taxi with her friends for the trip to the pier.

"Right on time," Carter greeted them from the deck of the *Gallant Lass*. "You're in the Plymouth Colony," he said to Leah and Raoul. He had named his staterooms after the first settlement in America. "You have the Jamestown and your young man is next door at Charles Town."

Stassney was glad her godfather was busy directing the loading of the baggage and didn't see her start or the fluttery clenching of her hands on her purse as she walked along the gleaming deck to her assigned room. The door to the Charles Town suite was open, and Paul stood in it, watching her approach as she came out of the companionway to the starboard side of the luxury ship.

"So, you did make it," he said when she stopped.

"Yes. So did you."

His lips curled in a half-smile that was more than a little cynical. "Didn't you think I would?"

She shook her head, and his eyes went to the swirl of ginger-colored hair as it settled back around her face. Involuntarily, his hand went to her temple to smooth it behind her ear. Setting his jaw with determination, he drew the errant hand back to his side.

"I wanted to see how the other half lives," he told her.

"You're being nasty," she said coldly, surprising him with the sharp reprimand.

"Carter Remington is the fifth richest man in the United States, according to *Fortune*," he said softly, watching her closely to see what effect his words had.

"So?" Her glance was oblique, her eyelids narrowed, a sign that she was truly angry, he was coming to realize.

His hand closed on the edge of the doorframe to keep from reaching out for her and pulling her into his room. He swallowed the sudden lump in his throat. "So, he's probably only twenty-five years older than you. That's not too much for a man with his kind of money. He'd be a good catch."

Her mouth actually dropped open. She could feel her jaw give way and her chin sag in total shock. Then she recovered. "I'm not going to dignify that with a reply," she said and marched on to her room, slamming the door loudly behind her. It was a full hour before she could trust her temper enough to change to shorts and a halter top and come out on deck.

Leah, Raoul, Paul and Carter were sitting under a cabana, enjoying the sights as they pulled away from Port Moresby, having to go first south then east before they could start on the northerly course that would take them back to Lyra. Stassney took the available chair between Paul and Carter, but she didn't look at the younger man. Instead she questioned her godfather about his various enterprises and asked after mutual acquaintances.

For the remainder of the morning, until lunch,

Stassney kept the conversation going, with Leah adding her share and Raoul tossing in bits and pieces, for he knew most of the people they spoke of.

Paul said little. Although he knew the names—they were all prominent in international news—he didn't know the actual people. Stassney and her friends obviously did. Strangely enough, he didn't feel left out but found the anecdotes interesting and amusing. His host was careful to include him by adding enlightening asides so that Paul could appreciate the finer points of some small joke. He had to admit that the older man was a decent sort of person.

After lunch, Stassney went to her room for her usual nap. It seemed normal to rest at that time in the tropics. The heat was enervating. The air-conditioned coolness of her room was restful. She felt her nerves relaxing, smoothing out like ribbons unraveling into long streamers. Today and tomorrow, she thought before she went to sleep. Would she make it with her temper intact?

At eight, they met in the main salon for drinks before dinner. Leah refused her favorite, kir royale, when Carter suggested it for her.

"I've sworn off alcohol for the duration," she said.

Stassney grinned, knowing she was talking of the confirmed pregnancy.

"The duration of what?" Carter asked.

"Leah and I are expecting our firstborn," Raoul

said, putting his arm around his wife's slender waist. There were congratulations all round and a toast, with milk for the mother-to-be and sherry for the rest.

"And when may I expect some grandchildren?" Carter demanded of Stassney when they were seated around the formal dining table a few minutes later.

Stassney choked on her soup. "Don't ask me questions like that when I'm eating! And give me a chance to get married first," she added peevishly. Then she smiled at her godfather with such sweet affection that it brought a mist to his eyes.

"Grandchildren?" Paul asked on a curious note, almost as if he were strangled.

"God-grandchildren?" Carter shrugged. "I'm not sure what they would be called. If I could talk her mother into marrying me, then they would be my grandchildren in fact. But I intend to claim them anyway."

Paul ate the delicious meal with absentminded attention. He ate or drank whatever was placed before him without being aware of what it contained. So the fifth richest man in the United States was her godfather...and in love with her mother. So he had made an absolute ass of himself again with her. Would she forgive him for his earlier insulting remarks? Would he forgive himself?

His dark blue glance went to Leah as the two women discussed names for the coming child, teasing each other with the ease of old and trusted friends.

"Raoul Rasputin," Stassney suggested, "You could call him Raspy for short. Or Rah-rah."

"I like that," Leah said, considering. They laughed.

Paul smiled at their quips, but his mind was on Stassney. He thought of how she would look with her small body enlarging with a child. The burning ache of desire settled in his lower body. His seed in her fertile warmth. Virgin warmth, he remembered. He would plant it so gently.

He went over the changes, seeing them in his mind's eye. Her pink-toned nipples would darken as life-giving blood began to flow to the child. His child. His body tightened painfully. Don't think it, he warned himself. Don't even think it.

He got through the reminder of the dinner and the evening by forcing himself to concentrate strictly on the conversation and not on the young woman who attracted him so mercilessly.

With the confidence of long association, Stassney led the way back into the main salon after the meal. Again the tray was placed in front of her and she served coffee or tea to the other guests. Her dress of emerald green came to a point deep between her full breasts and had transparent sleeves that were gathered into a ruffle at her elbows. She wore an opal pendant and earrings that flashed with green fire with each move of her head.

In spite of her anger, she was proud of Paul. She

could see that Carter liked the rather serious young man. There was a lengthy conversation between the three men about the gold and silver industries that were opening up in the island nation, and Carter explained his part in the economic growth of the area.

"I've always loved the Pacific islands," he said. "I was stationed in Hawaii when I was in the service."

The talk turned to world problems and the various hot spots of trouble. On this ship, sailing on a path laid down by the moon, Stassney thought the world and its problems far away. No wonder that people who came here threw over everything and never wanted to leave.

It was late when they said good night and went to their rooms.

"Stass," a deep voice halted her as she reached for her door.

Her back straight and stiff, she answered, "Yes?" coolly.

Paul stopped next to the railing, the moonlight bathing his lean, suited form in silver. He was aware that she had hardly looked at him all evening. Not that he blamed her after that earlier crack about her godfather's being a good catch.

"I owe you an apology," he started. With two long steps, he was beside her, his hands on her shoulders turning her to face him. He couldn't take her back another second. He pulled her to his chest, wanting her to warm toward him, to soften and melt into him. "Stass, I'm sorry," he whispered.

"That's perfectly all right," she said, a sure indication that it wasn't.

"No," he denied. "I was out of line...again. Please, I..." He could hardly tell her that he was excruciatingly jealous of anyone who came near her. He had no right to be, no right at all. Never in his life had he been so frustrated with events.

His hand smoothed down her back, and he found that the material of her dress had a slight texture like short velvet. He rubbed down it again. "Stass," he heard himself whisper urgently, hungrily. If he took her, she would be his. She had said so. The wanting of it was so great that he groaned deep in his throat.

Stassney sensed the conflict in Paul, the intense magnetism that pulled them together, the doubts that drove them apart. What was his problem? Was is that he still loved Anne and wanted her in place of Stassney? Did he feel guilty for the desire that he felt for Stassney, see it as a betrayal of his first love?

"Let me go, please," she requested.

"Kiss me," he ordered. His lips wrecked havoc with her control as he nuzzled the side of her face. "Stass, don't freeze up on me," he murmured, his hands doing exciting things along her back, her sides, her hips. How long would she stay before she grew tired of him and his passion and went back to her *real* life? Why think about it? Why not take what was offered and forget tomorrow?

Stassney fought against the rising sea of desire that rose and rose and threatened to engulf her senses entirely. She had told him how she felt, almost confessed in actual words that she loved him; did this mean he wanted her love?

His mouth found hers, and she was overcome with the magnificence of their passion, so wild, so tempestuous. His tongue probed, explored, found her inner softness and responding answer to him in her own gentle touches. She flowed into him.

"Stass," he sighed, lifting her into his arms like a prize of war and carrying her into her room. The door closed silently behind them, shutting out the world and common sense, shutting them in.

He put her down beside the wide, comfortable bed, not letting any space come between their bodies as he did. He wanted to crush her to him so tightly that she would become part of him, her flesh melding into his, so that she could never leave him. And yet, he felt so terribly gentle toward her, full of a deep *caring* that was unlike anything he had ever experienced for a woman.

His lips went to hers, and she accepted his kiss with a willing response, all her earlier anger evaporating in the heat of his caress. She sensed the desperation in him and wanted to hold him and comfort him for all the past disappointments in his life. Her arms encircled his shoulders, holding him as close as possible.

Their kiss went on and on, until neither of them could breathe, and they were dizzy with the rapture of it. Finally, Paul raised his head and gazed into her slumbrous eyes.

"I want to stay with you tonight," he murmured.

She wasn't sure what he meant. "Tonight?"

His tongue carved out fiery lines and curves along her neck and throat. "May I, Stass?" He spoke deeply, caressingly, and she wanted so much to say yes.

"I...I don't know. What are you asking, Paul?" She had to be sure that she understood his intent. Was he telling her that he loved her, too?

With stroking hands, he touched her body, roaming over her back and hips, along her sides. One hand slipped into the small space he allowed between them until he could cup her breast into his palm. Stassney gave a tiny gasp of pleasure.

"It's been ages since I last slept. Give me one night of rest. Let me lie in the sweet magic of your arms again."

She heard the seductive persuasion in his voice and knew she wouldn't say no to him. She had never loved like this before. It was so total, involving all of her. Parts of herself that she hadn't shared with anyone she now wanted to give to this man.

There was a tender smile in his eyes as he gazed down on her and saw the answer in her eyes. "Yes," he said.

"Yes," she echoed, lost in her love for him.

His hands went to the zipper of her dress, quickly

and expertly removing the garment as if he had undressed her a thousand times. A smile played over
his lips. In his dreams, he had done many things to
her, all of them pleasurable.

"Is this okay?" he asked, laying the dress over
the back of a chair.

Her slight nod brought him back to her side to
finish the task he had started. She had on one long
slip that was almost flesh-toned. His eyes darkened
to midnight blue as he slipped the straps from her
shoulders and peeled the clinging nylon from her
body. He disposed of her pantyhose and small lace
undies with an efficient motion.

"Where's your nightgown?"

She roused from her dreamlike state long enough
to indicate her suitcase. He got out a white silk
gown and lifted it over her head, pulling it down
her body, partially obscuring the tantalizing curves
of her figure.

Stassney wondered how long the gown would re-
main on and why he had bothered with it in the first
place. She found herself becoming impatient. She
wanted to rush ahead and know the outcome of this
night. A tinge of unhappiness added lavender to her
rosy view of the world. Would she want to go back
in time and take this night away when she woke in
the morning?

Paul lifted the sheet and his eyes invited her to
climb in. She did, her stomach muscles pulling in
with a convulsive movement of excitement. Then
he turned out the light and she heard him moving

in the dark. By silhouette, she watched as he stripped to his shorts and climbed in bed with her.

She trembled when his hands reached for and found her, bringing her against his strong length, holding her as he had done at the hut, with his body partially covering her in a protective manner.

"You make me feel...safe," she told him, realizing this was probably not the thing a lover cared to know.

He smoothed her hair from her temple, running his fingers into it to curve around her head. His mouth feathered tiny kisses along hers. "You are safe with me."

She tried to laugh. "Am I?"

His body was hard and tense against hers, his contours an exact fit for hers. She moved against him and felt the quick intake of breath that he drew.

"Do you trust me, Stass?" he suddenly asked in grave tones, as if some world event depended on her answer.

"Yes."

"Yes," he repeated slowly. "You have from the first. I can't figure out why." He sounded perplexed by this unearned faith.

"Because you're you," she answered. It was so simple. He was Paul, her love.

"Because you think you're in love with me..."

"I am in love with you." She settled herself more firmly in his arms, pressing her thigh between his.

"...and I can't take advantage of that love," he

concluded. With a heavy sigh, he began to extricate himself from her embrace. "Stass, let go. I've got to get out of here."

"No." She buried her face in his chest. "You said we could have an affair. I've decided that's what I want. We only have five weeks left."

He sensed the anguish hidden beneath her challenging words, and his arms clasped her to him, wanting to comfort her for the hurt he had already caused her. His selfish desire had only made things worse for her. Damn!

"Darling, it would never work," he whispered gently. "You come from a different world. Right now, this looks romantic and exciting to you, but six months or a year from now, you would hate it. And me. I couldn't take that, love."

She moved her head back, staring at his face so close beside hers on the same pillow. "Do you love me?" she asked in wonder and a growing hope. Maybe there was a chance, after all. With a knowledge all its own, her body moved against his, wanting him to complete the lovemaking he had started.

"I...what difference does it make?" he said. Taking her hands, he placed them at her sides and sat up on the side of the bed. "I didn't come on this cruise planning to make love to you, and I don't know why I suddenly thought we could just sleep together again. We've gone far beyond those two innocent nights at the hut, haven't we?" He rubbed his hands over his face wearily.

"Yes," she said, her heart going out to him in

his frustration. The attraction between them had been real and demanding from that first encounter. It had only grown with each new meeting. And hurt more with each parting, she added, a vague prophecy in the thought. "Sleep with me," she said.

"No!" He stood, searching around for his clothing without turning on the lamp.

"Not as a lover. Not even as a friend. We'll be two strangers, castaways on this luxury cruiser—we'll pretend it's an island—and we'll be lost from civilization forever." Her sudden soft laughter, seductive and cajoling, seemed to brighten the room.

He paused, considering her proposal, fighting the resurgence of raw desire.

"It's easier to be seduced, isn't it?" she asked, refusing to touch him and add to the flames.

"Yes," he muttered. He tossed his sock across the room and unfastened his pants, letting them drop back to the carpet. "Do you think we really will get any sleep?"

"Yes."

"Sometimes I don't know how to take you," he complained, once again nestled into her warmth, arms and legs entwined. Strangely, he experienced no flaming eruption of desire, only a sweet peace, as if passion had already been satisfied and he could now sleep.

"With a spoonful of sugar?" she suggested.

He kissed her soft, moist lips. "You're already sweeter than honey."

"Then with a grain of salt," she advised, her

spirit soaring happy and free. "I feel as if I just won some great battle." she snuggled against him, yawning widely.

"You did. The one against my better judgment."

She giggled. "I know. We're both insane."

He lay on his back with an arm around her, her head fitting into the groove of his shoulder. He kissed the top of her head. "I think you're right. I meant only to apologize to you for my crude remarks, then I got mad because you wouldn't look at me, then I was going to make love to you. But then I couldn't because you're sweet and innocent and are suffering from the delusion of being in love...."

She slapped him on his tummy for that insult, although she didn't take it seriously. She knew her own feelings.

"Did you ever consider that what you think is love is only moonlight in the South Pacific plus the circumstances under which we met? You were impressed with my TLC."

"I've learned a lot more about you since then. For one thing, you have a nasty temper. But I still love you." The words were easier to say this time.

He gave a little snort of disbelief, but he smiled in the dark. He was awake long after she went to sleep. He loved her, he admitted to himself, but that was one weapon he wasn't going to give to her. She would use it to get beneath his defenses totally. The contentment of holding her gave way to the deeper despair of knowing she would soon be gone.

Five weeks. It was only right for her to go back to her world—to what she really was.

Although she didn't have a fortune, she didn't seem to realize that a place in society could also be determined by upbringing and one's expectations of life. Stassney's were very high. She could easily marry into the wealthiest echelon of the world.

She shifted slightly, moving her leg up over him so that her thigh rested between his. He laid his hand on her side, caressing downward along the welcome weight of her leg. Awake, she was alert, energetic and determined; asleep, she seemed fragile and delicate.

She apparently thought she could have everything she wanted from life...including him. But he was older and wiser; he knew better. He knew about romantic dreams. And he had learned to deal only in harsh realities.

He drew her more tightly to him. Tonight was the dream, of course, but he would take it, this precious gift of having Stassney to himself for one perfect night. He slept deeply, peacefully, holding her all night.

He awoke with the dawn. He kissed her, his lips coaxing her awake and into awareness of him. He knew this was a dangerous time, that they were both vulnerable. He should quietly get up and leave her to her innocent sleep, but he continued to kiss her and to stroke her through the silk of her gown.

She responded naturally, her arms opening to receive him, caressing his back as he bent over her.

This was the last time he would hold her, he thought. He let himself go farther than he ever had with her, his hands moving under the silk to caress the satiny-textured skin of her body.

Removing the straps from her shoulders, he bared her breasts for his inspection, bringing a whimpering moan from her parted lips as he kissed the pink nipples that hardened with desire from his touch.

He put his lips against the spot on her throat and felt her pulse beating with a changing tempo as passion bloomed between them. "I love you," he murmured, realizing a second too late what he had said.

Chapter Eight

"Forget I said that." But the words, once spoken, couldn't be taken back.

Stassney touched his brow, caressed his cheek and chin, which were rough with morning beard. Her eyes gleamed up at him like agates. "Forget?" She shook her head.

Angry with his own clumsy declaration, Paul flung out of bed and began dressing. He cursed under his breath as he looked under every article of furniture for his missing socks. Finally he found them, pulling them on with jerky motions. He put his shoes on, too. Damned if he was going to be caught sneaking out of her room with his shoes in his hands like some kind of lecherous rake!

"Love is supposed to be a wonderful thing. Why do you act as if you had the plague?" she demanded, becoming irritated herself with his attitude.

"I should never have allowed it to happen," he growled, grabbing his shirt and turning his back to her while he tucked it into his pants and fastened the zipper and hooks.

She made a face of exasperation at his suddenly recovered modesty. Men!

Stopping at her door, suit jacket in hand, he glanced at her with a worried frown. "I didn't mean to hurt you, Stass. I never meant to do that." His eyes, deeply blue and as enchanting as a fairy tale, were truly apologetic.

"No, men never do," she said with the first real bitterness with life that she had ever experienced. She felt so strange, as if she had been cut off from her real self and were floating somewhere in space. This was a strange place to her—this place where she was loved but not wanted.

He hesitated, not wanting to leave her when she was so obviously hurt. "We're not right for each other," he began.

She gritted her teeth, knowing she was going to fall apart if he didn't leave soon. *WAGS always smile,* she reminded herself, getting out of bed and pulling her robe on. *Through heaven or hell or dark of night, WAGS always meet life with a smile and poise and the correct words for any occasion.* She made herself be calm. "Thank you for being honest with me. And for not taking advantage." *Always leave people feeling good about themselves.*

Confused, Paul stood at the door, studying her closely. She was tousled and undressed, but she acted as if she were ready for an afternoon tea. So maybe she wasn't hurt after all. He nodded once, not trusting himself to speak, and went out.

Stassney collapsed like a punctured balloon. She sat on the bed and, her eyes dry and burning, wished she had never met Paul Windham. She went into the shower and washed all traces of his touch from her body, as if he had left visible prints on her. She was definitely through with men, she thought. Then she cried.

"Come on, I have a surprise for you," Carter said after lunch. His steward had just told him his call was ready.

Stassney knew what to expect. She followed him eagerly into the radio room. Sure enough, her mother was on the other end of the satellite hookup.

"Yes, I'm having a wonderful time," she responded to her mother's questions. "My lungs are fine. I rarely cough now and have no trouble walking or climbing." She thought of asking for Band-aids for a badly cracked heart when asked if she needed anything. "No, we have stores here," she said, teasing gently.

"You've received calls from two big companies. Each of them wants you to come to their headquarters for an interview. Sounds like definite job offers."

Stassney didn't answer.

"Did you hear me? You have two..."

"Yes, Mother, I heard. I was just thinking." She

took a deep breath. There was no time like the present to make her wishes known. "Listen, I think I will be offered a lab position here in the islands. With the DLE. The Department of Lands and Environment," she explained to the silent transmitter.

Finally, "You would live there?"

"Yes, probably at Port Moresby on the main island."

"Why?" Mrs. Murdock demanded.

Stassney chose her words carefully. "It's like a whole new world here. The technological revolution is just starting, and I...well, I want to be in on it."

Her mother's sigh was audible, and her voice, when she spoke, had an edge of hardness. "You're like your father, always wanting some new adventure, some great challenge to pit yourself against. You had a secure job here. You could have taken over my position when I retired if you had applied yourself...."

Carter picked up the radio-phone. "You're not being fair, Elena," he said in the sternest tone Stassney had ever heard him use to her mother. "You did what you wanted, rising to the top of your field. Let the child do the same."

The crackling silence filled the room.

"Has she gotten involved with some man? Is that it?"

Carter glanced at Stassney. She shook her head. "No," he replied. "This is something she feels she should do. So leave her alone and let her do it."

There was an indignant gasp before Elena composed herself. "If I may speak to my daughter again? Stassney, I apologize if I spoke out of turn. I...I do want you to be happy, darling."

Stassney recognized the love and concern for her in her mother's voice. "I know that," she said warmly. She talked about the islands and the industries opening up and the skills she could contribute. Before they hung up, Elena gave her blessing, which made Stassney feel good about her decision.

"Is there a man?" Carter asked as they strolled the deck a few minutes later. His glance was kind.

She grimaced and shrugged. "Not right now. But I'd like for there to be," she admitted, grinning at him.

"Paul?" At her nod, he said. "A dedicated young man." His approval of her choice warmed her clear through.

"Well, he's honest, at any rate. He doesn't want to get involved. He seems to think I won't be able to take life here." She leaned against the railing, watching as Lyra grew from a misty dark shape into a tantalizing paradise of palms and jungle.

"And so you've decided to prove him wrong," he suggested shrewdly.

Her gaze darkened, went introspective. "I didn't think of it like that," she said slowly, sorting through her motives. "I was interested in the job before I realized I was in love with him. But I was attracted to him from the first." Her face was troubled when she raised it to him. "Paul said I was being romantic about life here; Mother said I was looking for adventure. Am I like that?"

Carter's face hardened. "A challenge is not the same thing as an adventure. Performing a task well is not the same as taking life on a dare. Don't let other people's views change your opinion of what you know yourself to be. I've never known you to behave in an irresponsible manner or fail to face facts."

His words were wonderfully reassuring to her. Pressing her face against his shoulder, she whispered, "Thanks, I needed that."

"We all need an occasional bolstering of our spirits when life slaps us down. Well, here we are," he said, bringing her attention to the docking procedure.

A few people from a coastal village watched the passengers get off. When no cargo was off-loaded, they went home. Stassney suffered a pang of sympathy for them. She, too, must get on with her life. She wasn't going to wait around for Paul to suddenly realize that he couldn't live without her. She listened with a polite attitude as he declined a ride back to the plantation, and watched without a change in expression as he picked up his suitcase and started along the dusty road in the opposite direction they would be traveling. She assumed he was going to one of his huts farther down the coast.

She, Leah and Raoul said good-bye to Carter. He had to get back to the States and declined an invitation to visit with them. They waved as the ship pulled away, then climbed into the blue station wagon so Sean could drive them home.

The trip up the mountainous ridges was much easier than her first time over those roads, but not as much fun, she thought. No mud. No lost purse. No tears of despair. No kisses at dawn. When they arrived at the house, she went straight to her room.

The next morning, she was up early, watching the sun rise and dispel the lingering mist from the humid air. Paul appeared on the path leading from the guesthouse, surprising her. She had thought he was at the other end of the island.

"Good morning," he said in distant tones.

"Good morning," she called softly to his back as he walked on without another word. In a few minutes, he went past in the station wagon with Sean. Probably going to inspect some crops. He didn't look her way when Sean beeped a friendly message on the horn. Sometimes it was very easy to hate the person you loved, she decided as she went in to dress.

"Shhh," Sean cautioned as he and Stassney crept as quietly as possible through the shadows under the trees.

More and more of her time was being spent in this man's company. During the past three weeks, he had taken her with him to all parts of the island as he went about the business of running a two-thousand-acre plantation that included seashore and mountain terrain.

He had shown her the tea being raised on the higher elevations, then the coffee and cocoa fields interspersed with some experimental gum trees. Next came large plantings of the winged bean on the level plateau, and finally, the coconut palms. A small citrus grove flourished in one valley.

"I hope they're still there. It's quite a sight," Sean whispered as they approached a noisy glen.

Stassney couldn't figure out what the odd, whirring sound was. Then she stopped dead still. "Ohhhh," she breathed. She stood transfixed, staring at the tree in the clearing. At first, her mind couldn't decide what she was viewing, then it came to her—birds of paradise!

At least two dozen birds were gathered in the tree branches, but not to roost. No, they were flying or leaping from one limb to another, displaying the most fantastic plumage she had ever seen.

"There must be a female nearby. These are all males, showing off for her, hoping she'll select him as her mate." Sean chuckled near her ear as they stood watching.

One especially bold male hopped out to the end of a branch. He puffed up a dark area under his throat and made a noise that was loud and rather musical.

"That's called his ruff," Sean explained.

The feathers above the ruff were iridescent green,

shining brilliantly in the sun. His head and back were a lovely shade of soft yellow. But the most striking aspect was the long red-orange feathers along his sides. He now lifted these in a proud show that brought a lump to Stassney's throat.

"That's his cape," Sean pointed out. "It's separate from his tail feathers. See the two long wires trailing out behind him? That's part of his tail feathers, which are shorter and hidden by the cape usually."

"He's beautiful. I'm already in love with him." Suddenly, she wanted the unseen female to choose this showy male. He seemed to be trying so much harder than the rest of the flock, his dance of courtship so earnest.

A second of stillness came over the group of flashing birds, then they rose and flew in different directions, disturbed by something unnoticed by Sean and Stassney.

"Do you think they saw us?" she asked, worried about the interrupted mating ritual.

"I don't think so. Maybe they decided it was time to go eat. We're late for lunch," he said, glancing at his watch. "Leah will be worried about you and angry with me for keeping you out all morning."

"She's been busy talking babies with Renata ever since we got back from Port Moresby." While Stassney thought babies were nice, she had been glad to escape the constant discussion of them between the other women of the island. Since it didn't seem to be her fate to produce any children—she hadn't been closer than a fleeting glimpse of Paul since that morning he had walked away from the cruiser—she didn't want to think about them.

"Yes," he said.

Her tender heart contracted in pity for this large, silent man who loved so hopelessly. Her pity got all mixed up for him and herself and the daring male bird who had performed for his love at the very tip of the branch.

When they arrived at the house, she touched his arm. "Thank you for taking me to see the birds, Sean. I'll never forget it."

His blue-green eyes were as lovely as the gleaming plumage, she thought, and so very gentle as he smiled at her.

"You're a nice companion, Stassney." His tone conveyed much more than the simple statement. "One a man could grow accustomed to having around. Paul's a fool." He bent and kissed her gently before leading her to the terrace where they usually had lunch. Leah and Raoul were waiting for them. The table was set for five.

"Where have you two been?" Leah demanded good-naturedly. "Doesn't anyone show up for lunch on time these days? It's almost one-thirty."

"Sean took me to see the birds of paradise. The males were showing off for a female. I think. We never actually saw her."

"Oh, Sean, you've got to take her to the mountains on the far side of the plantation." Leah turned back to Stassney. "The Crown Prince Rudolph's bird of paradise has been spotted over there. It's the most gorgeous thing you've ever seen in your life. And the male hangs upside down and spreads all his feathers out to attract a female."

"The males of various species in the animal kingdom willingly make clowns of themselves at the slightest encouragement from the females." Paul came up on the terrace from the path.

"And some need no encouragement at all," she said coolly, then wished she hadn't let him provoke a response.

Brown eyes clashed with blue for one brief second before Paul took his seat between Stassney and Raoul. He was so angry he thought he could shatter stone with the force of it. He had witnessed that tender kiss as he came up the path and had had to stop himself from forcibly interfering. But he couldn't prevent himself from wondering if Stassney were falling in love with Sean.

His gaze darkened as he sneaked a sideways glance at her, sitting so primly beside him, talking and eating as if she weren't driving him up the wall with her nearness. She was ripe for love, he thought. She was ready for it now as she probably hadn't been during her undergraduate days at college. Then she had been busy working and concentrating on her studies. But now, she was enlarging her life scope as she prepared to leave the confines of school.

His jaw took on a determined set. No one was

going to teach her about life…and loving…except him. If she were ready to experiment with her sexuality, then he was going to be her partner, not Sean. So she could just get that out of her mind!

"Do you want to go on a butterfly hunt tomorrow?" he heard himself ask, then groaned internally. No one would go when asked in that obnoxious tone of voice. "I thought you might be interested. We're going to try to start the ranch." He was gruffly apologetic.

"That sounds lovely," Stassney murmured after a slight hesitation during which she warred with her heart and lost.

"Hah!" Leah openly scoffed. Her glare at Paul let him know what she thought of his far-from-gracious invitation.

"Good, here's dessert," Raoul broke into the tension, sounding as if he thought everyone's disposition could use some sweetening.

The conversation drifted to other topics after that. Paul and Sean made plans to check on some irrigation canals that afternoon. Stassney asked a question about that and started an interesting discussion of the rivers and lakes on the islands which lasted until the two men got up to leave.

Paul touched Stassney lightly on the shoulder. "I'll pick you up at seven in the morning. We'll be gone most of the day."

"She'll need to eat and rest," Leah said, protective of her guest.

His eyes plumbed her depths as Stassney gazed

up at him. "I'll take care of her," he promised huskily, not taking his eyes from hers.

It was a long time after he left before she could breathe normally again and her pulse slowed to a less hectic pace. He was so totally unpredictable! And wonderful. And handsome. And so hard to understand. Why had he changed his mind about seeing her?

Leah excused herself after Raoul left, and went to her room to rest. Frowning thoughtfully, Stassney did the same. Lying on the boudoir lounge, she wondered why, after avoiding her for three weeks, Paul had suddenly invited her to spend the day with him. His tone had been harsh when he issued the invitation, as if he hated either her or himself for asking.

Her thoughts went to long ago, when she was nine and she had listened to her mother cry at night. Loving a man was hard. For the first time, she realized how Elena must have felt—alone, penniless, and with a child to raise. A lot of the joy had gone out of her mother at that time. Not that she didn't smile and keep up a brave front, but life must have seemed desolate at times. Jamie Murdock had been fun and exciting to live with. A light had gone out when he died, and no other man had rekindled it for Elena.

Tears formed in Stassney's eyes and slipped down her cheeks. She understood so much more now. A candle had been lit in her heart for Paul, and it would burn forever, but only for him. Only for him.

She was on the terrace, finishing her breakfast, when Paul arrived. He joined her for a cup of coffee, looking her over with approval as he sipped the hot liquid.

"You look delectable," he said.

Stassney glanced down at her cotton slacks, which were tan with yellow stitching. Her blouse was yellow, made like a bush jacket with pockets over each breast and a belted waist.

"That's the word Carter used. Delectable," she said, finding this somehow significant.

"Well, brilliant minds and all that," he teased, his gaze running over her, making her feel warm and beautiful.

It came to her that Carter and Paul were very much alike in many ways. There was a quiet seriousness to both men. And Sean, too, she honestly added. They were all examples of the type of man she preferred. Gentle yet strong, dedicated but fun, too. Not as cosmopolitan as Raoul or as flamboyant as her father had been, but with an equal charm. So it wasn't a case of "like mother, like daughter," in the choice of a man to love, she concluded, but she thought she and her mother loved in the same way....

"Ready to go?"

She answered Paul's smile with a radiant one of her own. Whether he wanted to love her or not, he did. And she loved him. And they were going to be together all day!

Paul helped her into the ute, fastening a rope for a seat belt across her lap when she was seated. "Aren't we getting modern?" she couldn't resist ribbing him about this latest acquisition.

"Don't want you falling out on your head," he replied equably. His eyes swept down her. "Or other parts."

She couldn't stop smiling as they ambled along over the rough roads, going deeper into the jungle terrain. Happiness shimmered on the air like sunlight on the dew-damp leaves. Birds sung an aubade, their morning song a greeting to the day. "Where are we going?" She really didn't care. She just wanted to hear his voice.

"To a distant valley." He laughed and, reaching over, ruffled her hair in a playful mood at odds with his attitude of the previous day.

"Will we see any birds of paradise, do you think?" She would love to see some of the different varieties that were supposed to live in the islands.

"Maybe." His grin disappeared and the harshness returned. "I wanted to show them to you. I spotted them when Sean and I were over that way a couple of days ago." He sighed. "But I waited too late to make up my mind about asking you. I thought it better…" He trailed into silence, deep in his own thoughts.

She forced herself not to be hurt as his silence told her of his doubts about being with her. "Is that why you asked me on this butterfly chase? You were afraid someone else would do it first?" There was a slight edge to her voice.

His glance was penetrating. "Yes," he admitted. "But I shouldn't have. And don't think it means more than it does."

Stassney did a fast burn on a short fuse, but she managed a saucy quip. "You just wiped out all your 'atta boys' for the next century. And maybe you had better take me back to the house. Today might be too much of a strain on both of us." A day in his exclusive company was no longer appealing. Not if he were going to resent every moment of it and keep warning her not to get her hopes up that it meant something lasting.

"Tell me that you weren't already thinking of what today might mean to *our* future when you agreed to come on this trip." He made a sound of disgust. "I know how women think, the romantic little daydreams that you use to snare a man...until you realize what life really is."

"I merely wondered why you asked after weeks of ignoring my presence," she said icily. Anne. He's thinking of his precious Anne. It wasn't fair to always be compared to the woman who had hurt and disappointed him. Couldn't he see they were two different people? And if he couldn't, wasn't she, Stassney, better off without him?

"Did you ever hear that when the first skins of the birds of paradise were shipped to Europe, the legs had been cut off? This led to the wide-spread belief that the birds lived forever on the wing—eating, sleeping and mating. The scientists speculated on this phenomenon and came up with the idea that the female laid her eggs on the male's back and incubated them there. Of course they were made to look like total imbeciles when the truth came out," he finished.

Stassney was silent, thinking this over. Finally, "What's the moral of this little parable? I'm sure there's a lesson for me in it."

He seemed to have difficulty speaking. His voice came out strained and husky. "This thing between us is a fantasy born of illusion. We had a hard time getting to the hut that day you arrived. Living through those two days together, well, it bred a closeness that isn't real. That sort of thing often happens to people," he explained patiently, teacher to slow student.

She wanted to tell him that he and Anne had apparently had a difficult time on her visit, and it hadn't brought them closer to each other, but she didn't. Turning toward him, she earnestly beseeched him, "But don't you see? That's natural. That's real. Your little history lesson, saying our feelings for each other don't have a leg to stand on, backfired." Her tone became loving and gentle as she teased him.

He didn't say anything for a long time. Then, "I saw that tender little kiss between you and Sean." He raised one dark brow expressively.

She wondered what he was getting at. "Yes, we kissed," she said quietly.

"If it's experience you want, then come to me, not him," he said, his smile sardonic.

Everything in her took offense at his implication that she was interested only in sexual gratification. "Do you think that's all I feel? A maiden's curiosity? I could have gone to bed with a different man every night of the week at school...if I had wanted to." Blinking away angry tears, she stared out the doorless ute, her arms folded across her hurting chest.

After a few miles of silence, he dropped over a sharp hill and into a small valley with a thin, misty waterfall at one end and a bramble thicket at the other. There was a profusion of flame-of-the-forest plants growing in the meadow next to the tiny creek. Wild flowers bloomed in the rainbow colors. Butterflies danced from one blossom to the next.

Paul parked at the edge of the stream where the road dipped into a shallow ford. Neither of them worried about other traffic as he stopped in the middle of the road. They sat in the vehicle for a few minutes without speaking.

"Stass," he murmured. "I'm jealous as hell. What can you expect from me when I see you kiss another man? I wanted to kill him, then beat you."

She raised and dropped one shoulder in a nonchalant shrug, refusing to care for his bruised feelings. "How do you think I feel each time you compare me to Anne?" Her eyes flashed to him. "If you don't want me, then you have no right to be jealous.''

"I've already told myself that. Well, come on," he said, as if resigning himself to whatever fate came along. "Look, let's just be friends today, okay?" He climbed out of the ute.

His seductive tone and cajoling look were more than enough to melt her heart, and she nodded solemnly. They grinned at each other, at peace for this moment. "What do butterflies eat? We'll look for their favorite plants." She grabbed the net and waved it around in the air, then started a search of specimens.

He looked pained at her ignorance. "They don't, usually. Their mouths are made for drinking." He gazed at her lips with longing, then went on, "And they sip nectar from the flowers. Some don't eat at all. The season for butterflies is short. Their only purpose is to mate and lay their eggs. Then they die. That's why it's all right to collect them after they lay the eggs.''

"I see. They die anyway," she said.

Seeing her mood become pensive, he lightened the subject. "Do you know what they were originally called? Bet you a piece of chocolate cake that you don't," he challenged.

"I don't have any cake," she reminded him.

"It's in your lunch."

"You get my cake if I can't tell you the answer?" She looked disgruntled about the whole thing.

"Yes."

"And if I do, I get your cake?" She wanted to be sure she understood the rules.

"Right." He was confident of his win.

She wrinkled her brow as if deep in thought, but, from the twinkle in her eyes, he had the feeling he had just been had.

"It seems I remember reading something one time...." she said.

"Do you know it or not?" he demanded.

"Flutterbyes?" she inquired sweetly, fluttering her lashes at him like mad.

He grabbed the book and started comparing its pictures with the insects in the area. "If there's one thing I can't stand," he mumbled audibly, "it's a know-it-all."

Stassney didn't answer. Her attention was riveted on a huge butterfly that she thought she recognized. When it waved its huge wings, she knew she did. "Paul, it's a birdwing! A birdwing!" She motioned for him to come over to the bush.

The giant butterfly was laying her eggs on the underside of a leaf, arranging them in a neat order. The couple watched as she finished and lifted away from the plant.

"Get her," Paul commanded.

"No, I don't want to. Let her go free," she pleaded.

Paul took the net and easily trapped the birdwing. "She's fulfilled her function, Stass. I need her to show to the villagers. This is one of the few bird-wings that they're allowed to collect.''

He returned to the ute where he opened a kit and removed a needle. Stassney watched him as he prepared a shot of ethyl acetate. He was obviously not used to syringes.

''Here, let me,'' she said after looking at the instructions. She quickly and painlessly injected the solvent into the thorax, and the butterfly immediately became still.

''That was well done.'' He replaced the needle and syringe in the kit along with the small bottle of liquid.

''I've done it before, except it was grasshoppers we were running some tests on.'' She saw the uncertainty in his eyes. ''Just because I suddenly went romantic and wanted to let her go doesn't mean I can't perform efficiently, if necessary.''

He carefully placed the insect in the paper envelope. Then he took Stassney by the shoulders. ''Stass,'' he began helplessly, not sure what to say. His callous netting had hurt her somehow, and he didn't know what to do about it.

''That's all right. You were doing your job. That's what this is—your job.'' She waved a negligent hand around to indicate the area. She stared at the ground at their feet.

''Hey, that's not fair.'' He lifted her face, studying her.

''I know,'' she admitted. ''But do we have to be practical every minute? I wanted to remember her as wild and unfettered. My first birdwing.'' Turning away, she brushed at her eyes, impatient with the emotion. Honestly, getting all torn up over a butterfly that would have died from a predator or naturally in a short time anyway. "Well, come on," she said on a forced note of gaiety. "The best ones are getting away."

But soon she was immersed in the task of finding, identifying and capturing both moths and butterflies. Paul found leaves with the chrysalis attached and clipped them for removal to a mosquito net at his house where he could wait for the adult to appear and then study its habits.

"Here's a swallowtail," she called, pointing to the distinctive points at the back tips of its wings. "A ulysses, I think." She checked the book again, comparing the blue and black example with the live specimen.

It was mid-afternoon before they stopped to eat. By then, they had a good number of perfect examples for the villagers to study. Paul had written (in a notebook) the type of locale and plant each one had been found on.

"Are you really going to eat two pieces of cake?" he asked wistfully, eyeing the wrapped slices which she had placed to one side of her sandwich.

"Umhmm," she said, licking mustard off her lips.

He looked so disappointed that she started laughing and nearly choked. She pushed a piece over to him. "Thanks," he said, opening it before she could change her mind. They grinned at each other, at ease due to the camaraderie of their work and the quiet peace of the hidden glen.

"There's a little pool near here about waist deep. Would you like to swim?" Paul was stretched out as far as possible on the seat of the Landrover.

"Is it safe?" She remembered the crocodile in the ditch on her first day.

"Yes, I think so." The words were drawled out lazily.

"I don't have a suit."

"Neither do I." He slowly turned his head and watched her as she wrangled with a decision. "It will be safe." His words were a pledge for his own behavior.

He climbed out and led the way around the brambles to a shallow bank. Keeping his back to her, he began to undress, leaving his clothing on a bush. She did the same. After they were in the water, they turned to each other.

"Nice, isn't it?" he asked.

"Like a bath," she exclaimed, delighted with the warmth when she had thought it would be much cooler.

They swam and played in the water like children, each happy for this moment, and gave no thought to tomorrow. It was on the way back to the plantation that Stassney realized the price would be paid for that perfect day when he dropped her off and said good-bye.

"When will I see you?" she asked with no shyness whatsoever when she stood on the steps to the house.

"I'll be busy, but I'll try to see you before you go," he said casually. Too casually.

"Oh." She couldn't think of anything else to say. So that was to be it. Just like that.

"The same arguments still apply." His skin seemed stretched tightly over his bones as the muscles of his jaw clenched then relaxed. "I live in primitive, even harsh, conditions, Stass. It just wouldn't work."

Her eyes seemed dark as midnight. "Thanks for a lovely day," she said politely and went inside.

Chapter Nine

The drums beat with an insistent call, now slow and steady, then speeding into a turbulent crescendo of sound before tapering off into a provocative rhythm. It was as if she were listening to the heartbeat of the jungle, Stassney thought as she put the finishing touches to her makeup.

Her outfit was simple but festive. She wore the island sandals Paul had given her, and a pair of black slacks with double pleats at the waist. Her long-sleeved shirt of Swiss batiste was smocked above her breasts and down each sleeve. Insets of Val lace edged each row of smocking and the long points of the collar.

"Time to go," Leah's voice called from the terrace.

Stassney's heart and the jungle drums went up in tempo at the same time. She rushed down the steps to the lower terrace where Raoul, Leah and Sean waited for her.

"I couldn't have planned this better myself," Leah said in satisfaction. "The singsing this weekend, then the farewell party Wednesday night to send you off in style Thursday morning." She sighed dramatically. "I can't believe how fast the time has flown. Can't you stay longer?"

"My apartment probably has a full community of spiders living in it that I'll have to evict, so I'd better get home and get with it," Stassney explained in serious tones. "And I want to get on with my project."

"You'll probably catch the spiders and take them to the woods to live," Leah predicted.

"Probably," Stassney agreed, laughing with the others. She took Sean's offered arm, and the two couples walked the half-mile path to the village. "What's the singsing in celebration of?" she asked as they went by Paul's home, which was dark. Was he at the village?

"Oh, Paul's new thing—the butterfly crop." Leah tossed off the information airily. "The villagers love the idea."

Sean spoke up. "It fits in with their life-style. Butterfly farming takes a lot of walking to locate specimens. The villagers are always on the jungle paths, either going to their gardening plots, visiting other villages or taking their produce to the native markets."

"Or checking out the cargo at the pier when

ships come in," Stassney added. A wistful expression flashed through her eyes and was gone.

"You're in for a real treat tonight," Raoul said as they neared the village where the party preparations were in full swing. "There'll be a style show such as you've never seen...."

'The men dress up for the women," Leah explained.

"Rather like the birds showing off," Sean elaborated.

Stassney's heart did a quick double beat in anticipation. She felt so oddly excited. Nervous and alert like a woods creature in a strange place, as if she had been transported by a magic wind and deposited in a place unknown and unfamiliar to her.

The head tribesman came forward with friendly dignity and welcomed them to the village. Stassney was surprised when she realized she understood most of what he was saying.

Glancing around at the rest of the men who were gathered into the village center, she thought Raoul and Sean were rather underdressed. The chief wore a long, decorated cloth suspended from his waist with brightly woven cord. Several necklaces, some of them made of dogs' teeth, were draped around his neck. His headdress was the most distinctive part of his costume. It was an elaborate concoction with a beaded headband and the gorgeous plumage of the bird of paradise. Feathers were also inserted through his nose, giving him the rakish air of a pirate with a strange mustache.

The women weren't as lavishly dressed. Their marks of beauty were patterns of tattooed scars on their faces.

The visitors were shown to their places, and they sat on tapa cloth mats which the women made from mulberry bark. Stassney eagerly watched the proceedings as other villagers arrived and were greeted. It was a large singsing. Two pigs were removed from the barbeque pit. Their jaws would soon grace the chief's hut to indicate his great wealth and generosity, Sean whispered to Stassney.

The guest of honor was escorted from the *house tamborana* and seated next to Stassney. Paul winked at her as he crossed his legs and sat Indian-fashion like the rest of them.

She thought he had never looked so handsome. He wore white slacks with a Hawaiian print shirt of royal blue with white flowers. Around his neck was a necklace of teeth.

He saw her eyes on it and lifted the ornament. "My gift from the tribe. Pretty, isn't it? If you're nice to me, I'll let you wear it sometime."

"I'm sure you wouldn't be able to part with it," she said, declining his offer and glancing up at him from under her lashes.

His chest moved in a sudden breath, as if his supply of oxygen had run out all at once. "You look beautiful." His knee moved until it brushed hers.

"So do you," she said sincerely.

"You're not supposed to return every compliment I give you."

"I can't help it."

They smiled into each other's eyes, then the smiles faded, to be replaced with a longing that neither could hide from the other.

"The sexiest mouth," he muttered.

"The most gorgeous eyes," she returned. Her laughter rang out at his exasperated expression.

"How have you been the past few days?" he asked. "Are you over your coughing spells?" His concern was real.

She nodded, tears filling her throat and making it impossible for her to speak. He hadn't come near her since the day of the butterfly hunt. The hurt of it was in her all the time, keeping her near the edge of tears, so that the slightest thing touched her heart, making it ache.

The feasting went on for hours. In addition to the barbequed pork, they had baked yams, steamed greens, breadfruit, coconuts, bananas and kiwi fruit. Platters of rice and bread were served.

"What's this?" Stassney asked, enjoying it all. She was eating a meat that tasted like ham.

"Smoked tree kangaroo," Paul told her after taking a bite.

Stassney looked faintly uncomfortable. "Is it really a kangaroo?"

He nodded, a lock of midnight black hair falling over his forehead. He brushed it aside. "Most of the land animals here are marsupials."

"Just like in Australia," she mentioned.

"Same original land mass," Sean broke into the conversation.

Stassney thought of the earth and its many changes through the eons. It seemed so miraculous. Everything seemed a miracle tonight, she thought. And anything seemed possible. Looking at Paul, she found him studying her with deep hunger visible in his eyes.

The night robbed the blue color from his gaze, but the firelight added sparks, as if a sparkler had been lit inside him. She knew her own eyes must be reflecting the same desire. A frisson raced along her spine as his hand caressed her there, rubbing up and down her back in short sweeps that started more fireworks inside her.

Later, there was dancing. The tall, hourglass-shaped drums beat out an irresistible rhythm which was picked up by the wooden tap of the split-gong. At some point, Stassney realized that the dancing was a courting ritual. As the hour grew later, couples slipped off, hand in hand, into the darkness.

The drums seemed to have invaded her blood. Stassney sensed the pervading beat in every cell of her body. Heat poured into her from the fire, from Paul's body and from his hand that occasionally caressed along her back.

"I'm ready to go home," Leah said with a yawn.

Raoul helped her up, then turned to the head tribesman and thanked him for having them at the celebration.

"This will be remembered as the year of the butterfly," Leah told Stassney as they started along the trail.

Glancing over her shoulder for one last sight of Paul, Stassney was startled to see him right behind her. Ten minutes later, she was filled with disappointment as he said good night and turned off toward his house. Declining a nightcap, then going to her room, Stassney changed into her gown and robe and sat down with her book. Soon the house became quiet and dark. From the jungle, the drums continued their muted symphony. Several troths had been pledged that night, she would wager.

She sensed his presence before his outline appeared through the sheer curtains at her door. She went out and stood beside Paul, both of them moving to the terrace edge. With hands on her waist, he lifted her to the rock wall. He sat next to her as he had at the singsing, close but not quite touching.

After several minutes of silently listening to the jungle serenade, he put an arm around her. She leaned her head into his shoulder, looking up at him with moonlight gleaming in her eyes. She let herself go a little insane. Moon madness. She wanted it to never end. "Paul," she sighed, wanting him.

His head bent to hers, his lips touching hers once, then again, and again, but without pressure. Then slowly, by degrees, he let the kiss deepen until they were both lost in the magic.

When he at last raised his head, he whispered, "Come on." Leading her by the hand, he took her into her room and turned out the lamp before laying her on the bed. Kicking off his shoes, he joined her.

"I love you," he whispered, "and it's tearing my heart out."

"What do you mean?" She kissed him eagerly along his neck and up to his chin, but he wouldn't let her reach his mouth.

He caught her roaming hands and held them in gentle captivity against his chest. "Carter Remington and I had a friendly little chat on his ship that morning before we arrived back here."

She closed her eyes in despair, knowing what was coming. Why did other people have to interfere in her life? She thought of herself as independent and capable; why did everyone try to protect her and take care of her?

"Lord, Stass," he said in a tone of amazement.

"Yes, I know." There was no emotion of any kind in her voice. "I told Carter if he willed his money to me that I would immediately give it to the Audubon Society or something like that. So he willed it to my children instead."

"With you and your husband as co-executors with a board of trustees. And with a very nice stipend to go along with it." His brief laughter wasn't amused. "The joke's on me, isn't it?"

"I never tried to fool you," she said defensively.

With a gentle touch, he smoothed the curtain of hair away from her temple and kissed her there. "If ever I entertained the notion that we might have had a chance, that talk effectively squelched it."

"Then why are you here?"

"Not very logical, is it?" he agreed with the unspoken accusation in her voice. "Tonight, sitting next to you, the drums and the tension in the air...I just had to hold you once more. Time is running out," he reminded her unnecessarily.

"Make love to me," she said, her voice going husky as the passion bloomed again in her and her heart raced with reckless longing. Against her, she could feel Paul's desire in every line of his lean, masculine body. He wanted her as much as she wanted him. Why couldn't they have this one pleasure? "Please," she whispered, burying her face against his throat.

"I can't, love. With your innocence and Carter's endowment, you can have your pick of all the men in the world. I won't take your gift from you."

She pulled herself from his arms, sitting up in bed with her knees hugged to her chest. "All the men...except the one I want."

He got up and paced about the room. "It would be great to be romantic about this—remember you asked if we always had to be practical?—but marriage between us would never work, Stass. We come from different worlds."

"You're at ease any place," she told him. "Here at formal dinners. Dealing with government officials. Celebrating with the villagers. Living in a hut. Don't use that as an excuse. I don't accept it."

"Then accept this: I am not going to live with you off the money you will, in effect, inherit."

"Is it really the money?"

"It's the life-style that goes with it, the one you're used to. And don't tell me how you worked your way through school. You have no idea what scrimping your way through life is."

Anger erupted in her. "And you're deciding my life for me, painting your own pictures of what it was and how it's going to be. Well, I'm not going to let you do that. No one tells me how to live my life, not you, not Carter, nor my mother!"

"Bravely said." He applauded her declaration.

Frustration with his attitude caused her to want to throw things at him, but she forced herself to patience. Acting like a spoiled child would only reinforce his opinion along those lines. "Your Anne must have really done you in."

"She married the wealthiest rancher in the district a month after she returned home. It didn't matter. I was over her by then."

Stassney shook her head. Turning on the lamp, she faced him. "You're never over the past if you let it warp your future." She held her arms out to him. "Don't let it ruin our life together."

He was torn by his desire to take what she offered for as long as possible and his determination to protect her from her own foolish actions. She didn't understand that it wasn't his past that was the problem; it was hers. Everything, he learned about her only pointed up that fact. "Stass, I don't want to hurt you...."

She closed her eyes. "Don't ever say that to me

again. Just leave…and don't come back.'' Her arms dropped helplessly to her sides, and she didn't look as she heard his steps, then the sound of the door opening and closing. After he left, she turned off the light and sat in the dark. It seemed easier to face life that way.

What was she going to do now? She had reached a point where she had to make a major decision in her life. What was it to be? Should she go back to the States, forgetting her love for Paul, and make a life for herself there? Sometime in the future, she might meet a man she could love enough to marry…or would she be like her mother, loving only one?

On the other hand, she could stay in the islands. The job offer had come through, and was just what she wanted—heading up a clinical laboratory under the direction of a world-known chemist. The pyrethrum flower was grown here. From it, the insecticide, pyrethrin, was produced. Her research would involve finding other natural pesticides and testing their effectiveness. She would probably have to work with Paul occasionally on field tests. Could she handle that? Her heart would ache each time he was near and break each time he said good-bye, but there were probably worse things in life…like never being in love at all.

On Wednesday, Stassney and Leah went to watch the gathering of the winged beans which were ready to be harvested. The men used both a small tractor for the job and hand-held scythes. The dried beans would be sold to a factory on the main island for processing into flour for humans and, with other ingredients, into pellets of feed for animals.

"I want you to take a nap so you will be rested for tonight," Leah said when they returned to the house.

"Yes, mommie," Stassney quipped.

"Get to bed before I spank you," Leah threatened.

Laughing, Stassney went to her room and rested for an hour before she got up and paced restlessly to the door and out on the terrace. The ridges to the west cast long shadows as the sun moved into late afternoon. From far away, she could hear the muffled noise of the tractor and an occasional shout from one of the men giving an order. On impulse, she walked down the path, stepped over the low dividing wall and went on along the trail until she came to the guesthouse.

Paul wasn't there. He was still in the fields, she thought. It would probably be another hour or more before he returned. He probably wouldn't show up for the farewell party that Leah was having for her. She walked around the perimeter of the house, finding a greenhouse next to the back patio. Curious, she went in.

There she found a variety of plants being cultivated. She leaned close to one vine and sniffed. Those were vanilla beans growing on it. There were other spices she recognized when she pinched a leaf or pod and released the odor.

"Finding anything interesting?" a deep voice asked.

"Are you going to have the villagers try growing these?" She indicated the spices and herbs crowded into the small space.

He nodded. "Roger and I want to set up a bottling plant to produce both extracts and dried herbs. Your godfather said he would provide an interest-free loan. Nice man," he commented.

"Yes, he is." She walked past him. His scent was strong and earthy from working outside. He had removed his shirt and draped it over his shoulder. His bare chest was streaked with dust and sweat. She longed to touch him.

The kitchen door was open, she noticed when she stepped out on the patio. Without asking permission, she went inside. In the middle of the vinyl-covered floor, she stopped and looked slowly around. Paul stood in the doorway, watching her.

Stassney tried not to feel anything, neither hurt nor betrayal, but she couldn't stop the churning of emotion in her. Anger became dominant as her brown eyes went from one object to another.

"This is really roughing it," she said in a choked voice, waving her hand toward the electric range top and built-in oven, the microwave oven that occupied one section of a tiled countertop, and the refrigerator-freezer neatly fitted into ceiling-to-floor cabinets on a wall of its own. Reaching into the

handy ice cube container, she removed several of
the frozen crescents and pelted him with them.
They struck his chest and fell harmlessly to the
floor.

His face went dark as thunder.

With a little cry, she turned and fled, but he
caught her before she could reach the door into the
hall. He yanked her against him, lifting her high in
his arms. Going down the polished hallway, he
turned right into a bedroom. There he dumped her
on the bed, his face grim with anger. He stood over
her for a second, breathing heavily, as if he had just
completed a marathon, then he tossed his sweat-
soaked shirt aside and threw himself on her, taking
his weight on his arms, but effectively pinning her
under his hot, work-weary body.

"I ought to take you just to teach you a lesson
about invading other people's homes."

For the first time, Stassney knew real fear of him.
He was so angry with her. She could feel it in the
tremor that ran through him as he held her captive
with his body. She could see it in the set of his
mouth and fierceness of his eyes as he glared down
at her, only inches from her face. She could hear it
in the labored rasp of his breath through his parted
lips.

"Paul," she began hesitantly, hating the concil-
iatory tone in her voice.

"Shut up," he said succinctly. "You're just like
the rest of the women Leah has had visit her. You
think just because you want a thing, then it should

be yours. You push your way into a man's arms, his heart and his home, and give no thought to what you're doing to him, what emptiness he'll live through when you're gone. Do you think women are the only ones who suffer from a bad love affair? Do you think you're the only ones who hurt?''

Tears formed in her eyes and rolled unheeded down into her hair.

He rolled off her and flung an arm over his face. ''Yes, cry. Let's have the whole repertoire of persuasion.'' His voice was so bitter.

Fresh tears streamed from her eyes. Turning, she pressed her face into the pillow, trying to compose her flayed emotions. There was nothing she could do to comfort him…or herself. Sniffing and wiping at the moisture on her cheeks, she got up to leave.

''Why did you have to come here?'' he demanded tiredly. ''Now I'll see you here all the time, not just in my dreams.''

''I'm sorry,'' she said.

''Sorry doesn't get it,'' he retorted, throwing her apology at her. As she spun from him, his arm shot out and grabbed hers, pulling her down beside him. His eyes looked deeply into hers; then he closed them, as if he couldn't bear to see her pain. His hand stroked her shining dark-ginger hair. ''Don't cry, Stass. Don't cry.''

''I…I won't.'' She gulped back the surging tears, squeezing her eyelids as tightly together as possible.

Their mouths searched for one another, meeting

in an exchange of consolation for past days...and nights...of misery. The kiss was endless. Neither of them wanted to stop.

His hands caught her around her waist and he moved her until she lay over him, her full breasts pressing against his chest and eliciting a growing ache of need from him. "I need you," he murmured, bestowing kisses in a burning path along her throat. "I need you so much, I think I'll die from it."

"I need you, too." She was mindless with the joy of being in his arms once again. This was where she belonged. She knew that as well as she knew the sun would rise in the east and set in the west—an irrefutable fact of life. "Oh, love," she moaned, wanting everything from him.

With a movement of his lithe muscles, he turned them to lie side by side, his arms holding her crushed to him as if he would absorb her essence into himself. "Each day without you is longer than the one before," he complained in loverlike accusation, his lips toying with hers, pressing, retreating, tasting then covering them in a kiss of deep yearning.

Her hands roamed at will over his back and along his sides. She explored the muscles of his shoulders and the cords along his neck. She ran her fingers along the slight indentation of his spine and along the rising curve of his hips. She marveled over the rock-hard strength of his thighs, which seemed so much stronger than her own. "You're so strong," she told him, letting him hear the wonder in her voice and see how taken she was with his masculine handsomeness.

"You're so perfect." He took her breast into his hand, cupping its fullness briefly before going to the buttons on her blouse. Unfastening those, he pushed the cotton to each side of her, watching as her nipples contracted beneath the knitted tricot of her bra, the pebbly outline plain for him to observe. He laughed softly.

She smiled at his loving play, glad to bring him joy, happy to see the shadows erased from his beautiful eyes, which gleamed on her with hungry anticipation. A tiny thrill ran though her like a jolt of electricity. She felt as if she would burst if he didn't make love to her completely and immediately.

"Darling," she murmured. "Oh, darling. It'll be all right. You'll see. Everything will be wonderful." She thought of their future together, both of them working at interesting careers that were closely related. It would be... "Heaven," she said, running her fingers through the damp hair on his chest.

With sure fingers, Paul opened the hooks on her slacks and pushed the zipper down. Sliding down her body, he kissed all the area around her navel, then tickled her with his tongue until she was laughing and squirming in his arms.

"I like the sound of your laughter," he said, coming back to her lips.

"A happy sound," she told him, grinning at him

with some of her former impudence. He continued to look at her lips as his face grew thoughtful. Slowly, his hand came up and he caressed her lower lip, teased the corner of her mouth, then outlined her upper lip. Gently, he reached up and flicked her nose, then tested the length of her eyelashes.

With a premonition, she noted each of his actions. It was as if he were memorizing each part of her so that he would have a clear picture when she was gone. "No," she protested agonizingly. "You can't do this to me again. You can't pull me to you and then push me away like this. I won't let you." Her arms closed convulsively around him.

"Don't make it harder for us," he said in the gentlest tones...and the saddest. His hands rubbed up and down her sides.

"I'm not. You do that all on your own."

"I don't want to hurt you, Stass."

"Then don't. Just hold me." Her eyes challenged him. She was steadfast in her belief in their love.

He shook his head, refusing her. "You think that love will solve all our problems, but, sweetheart, it won't. It only covers them in stardust for a while. And what happens when that wears off?"

"We go on with our lives, loving each other on a new level." She was sure of this one thing.

He sat up on the side of the bed, holding her and rocking her back and forth. She gave him tiny kisses all along his throat, stopping to feel the pulse that beat heavily in the groove over his collarbone. His defenses were crumbling with each touch of her mouth on him. If he didn't get her out of the house soon, there would be no going back. All of his protective feelings for her were being drowned in a deluge of passion. When she lifted her head, his mouth went instinctively to hers, covering her soft lips in a kiss that admitted there was to be no retreat for either of them. He pressed her back into the covers.

"Hey, boss," a voice called from outside the door.

The couple on the bed stiffened. Paul fought a groan of protest as he forced himself to sit up. "Yeah, man?" His intent gaze saw the flush of embarrassment on Stassney's face as she straightened her blouse and fastened her slacks.

The field foreman wanted to know if they should service the tractor and take it to another field for tomorrow's work. Paul said that would be good. "I'll see you there in the morning."

"Right, man." The foreman left for his home.

"Saved by the bell, as they say," Stassney said in strained tones. She looked anxiously at Paul, wanting him to take her back into his arms and finish his lovemaking. And to tell her that he loved her and wanted her with him every moment from now on.

"Yes." He ran a hand through his hair. "You'd better get back to the main house."

"Is that all you have to say?" She couldn't believe him.

"Yes," he replied.

They both stood, she to leave, he to go take a bath. She looked at him once more in disbelief, then whirled and ran out of the house and up the path to Leah's house and the safety of her room. She still had to bathe and dress for the party that night. She had never felt less like having fun, she thought as she went in and closed the door behind her, panting only slightly from her exertion.

Chapter Ten

"That is the most beautiful dress I've ever seen," Renata, resplendent in black lace, exclaimed upon greeting Stassney that night. "What is this color?" She fingered the satin skirt that draped from the waist to the floor. The strapless bodice was formed by ruffles of the material rising from the waistband like petals.

"Kim calls it mulled wine, but I think it's more like cranberry," Stassney said, glancing down at the fitted satin bodice that cupped her breasts from a low vantage point, pushing them into enticing crescents. The dark red, almost wine, color brought out the dark red in her hair. With her skin tanned a deep gold, she looked the picture of radiant womanhood.

"It's dark cherry," Leah said decisively.

After the Joliquins moved on, Stassney greeted

the other guests, people whom she had met during her island stay. She smiled and smiled, for hours, it seemed. Finally, everyone was there, and she was free to move about the large orchid-decorated salon. She spoke cordially with everyone, recalling some pleasant occurrence she had shared with each person, making each feel that he or she had been an exceptional host or hostess.

When Paul came in through the terrace doors and spoke to Leah and Raoul, Stassney noted the fact. He wore his white jacket and dark pants, which seemed the usual dress suit for the men she had met here in the islands. Although she didn't look directly at him, she was aware of his gaze sweeping the room until he found her. Only her heart missed a beat at that moment. Outwardly she went on with her conversation with the government administrator who was in charge of affairs on Lyra.

An hour later, throat parched, she went to the refreshment table. She smiled at Leah's major-domo, who was acting as bartender and prepared her glass without asking what she wanted.

"What are you drinking?" Paul asked, coming up behind her.

She was ready for him. Turning, she smiled her best society smile, which held just the correct amounts of warmth and reserve. "A Stassney royale," she told him truthfully.

"I'll have the same," he told the bartender. "What is it?" His questioning glance went to the lovely creature whose beauty rivaled any bird of paradise he had ever seen.

"It's champagne with a touch of fruit-flavored liqueur."

"Unusual name," he commented, accepting his glass. Raising it slightly, he toasted her silently, then sipped the golden liquid. "Orange liqueur," he decided.

"Yes. Sometimes I like it with coconut or cherry or banana flavors. The wine steward at a restaurant in New York created it for me when Carter took me there for my twenty-first birthday," she explained the name.

"That figures," Paul said, a sardonic twist to his smile.

"Excuse me, but I think I should circulate." She laid a hand on his sleeve briefly and moved away in a flutter of lace and satin, so graciously feminine that every eye was drawn to her.

The evening moved toward its inevitable end. Stassney received invitations from all the guests, asking her to return and stay with them in the future. She returned handshakes and kisses with unfailing charm as she bid each person farewell. Finally there were only household members left. And Paul.

"Oh, I'm dead," Leah declared, falling into a deep chair in the study in a heap of blue tulle. "Let's have something to eat. I can't remember whether I ate anything or not."

Small cups of chocolate were passed around plus

plates of leftover treats from the party. Stassney absently ate kiwi fruit covered in powdered sugar. Conversation was sporadic, mostly about the harvest. At a yawn from Leah, Sean immediately stood and wished them all a good night.

Paul, too, stood. He looked at Stassney. "I have a going-away present for you. I probably won't see you before you leave tomorrow," he explained at her slightly surprised expression.

"How thoughtful," she heard herself say as she accepted the small box. She knew the gift was a piece of jewelry. Although she knew he wouldn't— surely he wouldn't!—give her a ring in front of everyone, still her heart beat faster as she removed the lid. Inside was a tiny gold butterfly suspended on a chain as fine as a thread.

Please, don't let me cry in front of everyone, she prayed. The tears—hot, heavy and hurting—pressed against her eyes, and just for a second, the delicate gold filigree blurred disastrously. *Through heaven or hell or dark of night,* she repeated rapidly to herself several times. Looking up, she smiled warmly. "Paul, it's lovely. Each time I look at it I'll remember our butterfly hunt. I still think a butterfly ranch sounds like an impossibly romantic idea!" Her laughter tinkled softly across the silent room, as charming as a wind chime. She was doing well, she thought.

Her composure didn't waver as she met the pity in Leah's eyes. Still smiling, she stood, and lifting herself on her toes, she kissed Paul's cheek. "Thank you," she murmured.

Sean came over and kissed her, then left the room. Paul said good night and went on his way. Calm and serene, Stassney excused herself, refusing Leah's invitation to stay and talk about the party the way they used to do as girls. She felt she was beyond that now. This was a woman's hurt and not to be shared at this moment. She went to her room, and not once did she cry.

Stassney sat on her suitcase at the pier, waiting for the ship to arrive and take her away. She had insisted that only Sean drive her down and then leave her. She wanted to say good-bye to the island in privacy. Leah had understood, and Stassney had finally convinced Sean that this was what she wanted. Besides, she would be coming back in a few weeks to Port Moresby. She would see them again soon.

Out in the lagoon, she could see some of the coastal villagers on a *lakator*, a huge, flat raft, from which they were fishing with nets, probably using derris root, which paralyzed the fish for a quick catch. She wondered if the powdered root were harmful and if the method were illegal. So many things to learn about a new place, she thought.

Down the beach, she could see a family working together. They were opening coconuts and laying the meat out to dry in the sun. The father, mother and three small children were busy, yet there was much laughter between them and lots of little touches, she noticed. The family units formed the building blocks of civilization, she realized.

Her mind roamed without conscious direction to more basic combinations of life than the family. She considered the atom and its combining properties, especially hydrogen and carbon. Those two elements formed the basis of the entire field of organic chemistry...of life itself. From basic hydrocarbon-molecules, nature and chemists formed alcohols, aldehydes, acids, and those most important compounds—the amines which formed all living protein.

How had it happened, that first speck of life, the separation of one molecular chain into two identical ones? From that fragile beginning had grown this, she thought, looking again at the family and then the fishermen, all working together. The miracle of life, she thought, watching the young mother on the beach lift her smallest child to her breast to suckle.

Looking back toward the jungle—all that wild growth!—she watched a yellow butterfly, looking like a slice of solid sunshine, lazily circling a flower. It lifted on the breeze and came toward her. She raised her hand, and for a minute, she thought it was going to land, but again it changed its mind and fluttered away. Slowly she let her hand fall to her lap. She had had her season for butterflies; now it was time to move on. She turned back to the sea, but for a long minute, all she saw were shades of misty blue.

"Where is she?" Paul burst upon the terrace where Leah was going over her household accounts. He was hot and breathless from running.

"She's gone."

"Gone? She can't be. It's not time," he protested, glancing around as if he thought Stassney were hiding from him.

"She wanted to go down early...to commune with nature or something like that," Leah said.

He smiled. "Yes." In his mind, he could see her standing on the pier, saying good-bye to the island. "I've got to stop her." He ran for the front of the house where the ute was parked.

Leah dashed after him. She grabbed his arm before he could start the engine. "What are you going to do?" she demanded, all fierce concern for her friend.

"Ask her to forgive me. Beg her to marry me," he replied. He turned on the switch and the Landrover roared into life. He grinned at Leah's shocked face, then they looked at each other solemnly.

Leah spoke. "She's a special person. She doesn't realize it, but she is."

He nodded. "I know that." His expression became gentle. "Don't worry, I'll take care of her from now on."

She stepped back, smiling. "Good luck."

"I think I'm going to need it." He put the vehicle in gear and started off down the mountain to the seacoast.

Stassney heard the straining of the engine before the auto came into view. She shook her head. She had probably forgotten something and Leah had sent Sean hurrying back down to bring it to her. Whatever it was, it couldn't be worth risking life and limb for. She would reprimand Sean for his maniacal driving, she decided.

The ute came around the bend in a cloud of dust and careened to a stop next to the wharf. Stassney's face became expressionless as Paul jumped out and ran toward her.

"Here," he said, panting.

She took the note he handed her and glanced at it. There was a column of numbers, each number neatly labeled: Salary, Savings, Investments, Life Insurance. She looked up. "What is this?"

"It's a statement of earnings and what I'm worth." His eyes roamed over her face anxiously. "If you think you can live with what I can give you...." His voice trailed off and the question was asked by his gaze.

"Is this a proposal?" she asked. She wanted to be sure she wasn't jumping to conclusions.

"Yes." Then he grinned at her.

Her mouth compressed into thin lines. She gave him her mad-as-hell look, which he immediately recognized. He groaned audibly. He had handled it all wrong, he realized too late. She didn't care, and had never cared, about money.

"This is what I think of your paltry proposal!" With precise movements, she tore the paper into shreds, which she tossed into the breeze. His offer of marriage became a stream of confetti that settled into the sea.

"Stass," he began, speaking tenderly as if to a child.

"If you think I'd accept a lover who was so lily-livered that he wouldn't accept a totally free gift of love, you can think again. Everytime I'd have a sad thought or got mad or frustrated, you'd think I was regretting the marriage. No thanks, I don't want that kind of a life." And she turned her back on him.

Two villagers ambled onto the pier. Paul pointed to Stassney's luggage and then the ute. "Load'm you that, okay?" he requested in island vernacular. Then he swept his stubborn woman into his arms and carried her to the ute, tossing her in and tying the rope across her lap in spite of her hindering hands.

He drove off with a wave and to several bits of shouted advice from the two men. Laughing, he headed for the hut. Stassney glared at the road in stony silence.

When he pulled into the clearing on the ridge, she spoke. "You are making me miss my boat." Its whistle could be heard as it approached the landing at Lyra.

Paul untied the rope and lifted her out. Guiding her with a hand on the small of her back, he helped her up the steps and into the kona-grass hut where they had first stayed together.

"When you're ready to leave, I'll order a seaplane," he said huskily. Now that he had her there, he wasn't sure how to proceed. It certainly would have been easier in caveman days, he admitted wryly. But he didn't want to overpower her. He wanted her to come to him as she had before...when he had been too stupid to accept her gift of love.

"I'm ready."

"No." He couldn't let her go yet. "Stass, I was wrong about us. I love you and I want to marry you."

She faced him. "Why the sudden change of heart?"

"I talked to Roger Natim. He said you had accepted a job, that you would be coming back."

"I did. I am."

"Because of me?" he asked.

"No! Because I *want* to. I'm interested in the things that are happening in this part of the world. I want to be a part of it, too." She looked down. Total honesty demanded that she tell the total truth. "And maybe you were a factor in my decision, but not the only one." She shrugged helplessly.

"It's the same for me," he explained. "I was considering finding something back in the States when my contract ended here. For you. Then when Roger said you were coming back, I realized that you and I were perfect for each other."

She stared at him, puzzled by what seemed obvious to him.

He caught her shoulders in loving hands. "Don't

you see, darling?" he asked softly. "We were each willing to go to the other, to adjust our lives for the one we love. What can be greater proof than that, that we're perfect for each other?" he ended on a reasonable note.

Stassney touched his cheek. "Were you really thinking of coming back to the States for me?" Her eyes were filled with wonder.

"Yes. I'd go anywhere for you. I can find work in my field in many places, but only with you can I find my love." He was so sincere that she couldn't doubt him.

Her gentle gaze probed deeply into his beautiful blue eyes, and he let her enter into his thoughts as much as she wanted. "You have a nasty temper, but I love you anyway," she at last murmured.

Drawing her to his chest, he kissed along her forehead and down toward her mouth. "Is that a firm maybe?" he asked lightly, feeling a fierce rush of love and desire for her.

"It's a definite yes," she whispered softly.

With a joyous whoop, he lifted her into his arms. His lips did ravishing things to hers, and she responded fully to each passionate overture.

"Stass?" he questioned, not wanting to push her into anything.

She had no trouble with doubts or modesty or any of those feeble qualms. "Yes, love," she answered.

He carried her into the small, stark bedroom. Letting her stand, he kissed her with a thoroughness that robbed her of breath. His hand touched just under her breast, feeling the quickening beat of her heart. "Sure?"

"Umhmm," she said.

He slowly, lovingly removed her skirt and blouse, her hose and wedge-heeled sandals. When she stood before him in only panties and bra, he paused to admire his treasure. With quick, impatient movements, he threw off his shirt and jeans.

But when he reached for her again, all his actions were controlled and careful. He turned her around and unclasped the bra fastening. He slipped her underpants down over her hips.

"Sit," he said, and she did. He smiled, remembering his first night with her. He tossed the bit of nylon to the wicker chest. Naked, he sat beside her, his hands going to her smooth skin to caress all its bare, inviting surfaces. "I love you," he whispered, assuring her.

Stassney had never felt so happy and so secure. There was no fear in her, only the confidence born of trust and love. "I love you, too."

He kissed her for a long time before proceeding. He made sure she was comfortable at each stage of his seduction before he went to the next. Her warm response assured him that his touch was welcome. When at last he laid her down on the tapa cloth mattress, she opened her eyes and gazed at him with a look of pure happiness.

"You've always trusted me," he said hoarsely. "From the very first." He kissed her neck just below her ear. His voice was a whisper. "Do you know what that does to a man to be so trusted?"

"N-no," she said with a little catch in her voice. His hands were doing marvelously exciting things to her breasts, rubbing the pointy tips gently, then squeezing the entire globe with fondling motions. Heat was spreading throughout her body.

He stirred the flames of desire by moving seductively over her before touching her face with one hand. "It makes me want to do great deeds for you so your eyes will always light up the way they do each time you see me."

Her lashes drifted down over her revealing eyes.

"No, don't look away," he pleaded softly. When he gazed once more into her lovely brown eyes, he continued, "But trust also brings the responsibility of protection with it. I wanted to guard your romantic illusions, beloved. I didn't want you to be disillusioned with life...or with me. I couldn't bear to see hate in your eyes...."

"You won't, not ever," she said. Her hands began a pattern of roaming as she explored his body with increasing ardor.

His breath caught in a small gasp. His love combined with an equal measure of longing, and he knew he wouldn't halt this time unless she wanted him to. He kissed her again and again and felt her move instinctively beneath him, using a woman's eons-old knowledge to let her lover know she wanted him. "Stass," he whispered, letting her see how much he wanted her.

With his hands and lips, he brought her to the highest point, then slowly merged his desire with hers. For long minutes they rested; then he felt her move against him. He smoothed the hair from her temple and kissed her there before moving to her waiting lips. "Ready?" he asked, knowing that she was, wanting to tease her a little before going over the edge into ecstasy.

Stassney experienced the building tension as a series of steps, each one leading to a level more intense and exciting than the last. She was totally involved with what was happening to them. The basic elements, she thought. Male. Female. Life.

"Paul, my love," she whispered, yet it was cry. "Oh, love." She held him tighter and tighter, her body arching under his, meeting him with equal need and then finding the satisfaction of love's reward, that wonderful peace and closeness at passion's end.

Paul heard her cry and let himself follow. Together, in each other, they found the final bliss. He turned them, tucking her against him as he had before, but this time it was so new.

"Feeling married?" he asked in a lazy drawl.

"Feeling happy. Contented." She rubbed her hand over the pelt of hair on his chest. "Feeling loved."

"You are." He caught her hand and kissed it. "Where do you want to get married? In Connecticut?"

"Would that be possible?" she asked.

"Yes, I have several weeks of vacation due me. I thought I could fly in for your graduation, then we could get married and have a honeymoon trip on the way back here."

"Sounds heavenly." She yawned sleepily, wanting to stay here in his arms forever.

"Listen, Stass. If you ever want to go back home to live, just say the word. We probably will when we have children..." He stopped abruptly, gazing down at her as she opened her eyes. "Stass, I...I forgot.... All my fine talk about responsibility and I forgot." He was angry with himself. "I said I'd take care of you."

She laughed. "It should be all right. If it isn't, well I'll let you know."

He planted kisses along her cheek, tormented the corner of her mouth. His hand touched her throat, finding the tiny necklace there. He moved it aside to kiss her.

"I thought I would never see you again. I nearly cried when I opened your gift and found the butterfly inside. I knew it meant good-bye," she confessed.

"Not good-bye," he said huskily. "For us, butterflies mean forever." And he sealed his pledge with a kiss.

*   *   *   *   *

SPECIAL EDITION

Stories of love and life, these powerful
novels are tales that you can identify with—
romances with "something special" added
in!

Fall in love with the stories of authors such
as **Nora Roberts, Diana Palmer, Ginna Gray**
and many more of your special favorites—as
well as wonderful new voices!

Special Edition brings you
entertainment for the heart!

SSE-GEN

SILHOUETTE®
Desire®

Do you want...

Dangerously handsome heroes

Evocative, everlasting love stories

Sizzling and tantalizing sensuality

Incredibly sexy miniseries like **MAN OF THE MONTH**

Red-hot romance

Enticing entertainment that can't be beat!

You'll find all of this, and much *more* each and every month in **SILHOUETTE DESIRE**. Don't miss these unforgettable love stories by some of romance's hottest authors. Silhouette Desire—where your fantasies will always come true....

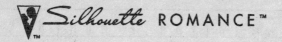

Silhouette ROMANCE™

What's a single dad to do when he needs a wife by next Thursday?

Who's a confirmed bachelor to call when he finds a baby on his doorstep?

How does a plain Jane in love with her gorgeous boss get him to notice her?

From classic love stories to romantic comedies to emotional heart tuggers, **Silhouette Romance** offers six irresistible novels every month by some of your favorite authors! Such as...beloved bestsellers **Diana Palmer, Annette Broadrick, Suzanne Carey, Elizabeth August** and **Marie Ferrarella,** to name just a few—and some sure to become favorites!

Fabulous Fathers...Bundles of Joy...Miniseries... Months of blushing brides and convenient weddings... Holiday celebrations... You'll find all this and much more in **Silhouette Romance**—always emotional, always enjoyable, always about love!

WAYS TO *UNEXPECTEDLY* MEET MR. RIGHT:

♡ Go out with the sexy-sounding stranger your daughter secretly set you up with through a personal ad.

♡ RSVP yes to a wedding invitation—soon it might be your turn to say "I do!"

♡ Receive a marriage proposal by mail— from a man you've never met....

These are just a few of the unexpected ways that written communication leads to love in Silhouette Yours Truly.

Each month, look for two fast-paced, fun and flirtatious Yours Truly novels (with entertaining treats and sneak previews in the back pages) by some of your favorite authors—and some who are sure to become favorites.

YOURS TRULY™:
Love—when you least expect it!

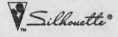